Honey, I'm Hired!

I saw the faint gleam of light on white, white legs curving deliciously down from a man's coat. My coat. Her two hands held the coat together in front. And above it was the gleam of long blonde hair, the blur of a lovely face.

"Well, hello!" I said.

She reached for my hand and accidentally grabbed the gun and let out a squeal and I almost emptied that gat into the air, whooping like an Indian.

She said rapidly, "I'm about to die. You are Sheldon Scott, aren't you?"

"Shell. Call me Shell. That's me. Well, this is . . . a pleasant surprise. How the hell do you happen to be here?"

In a fast rush of breath she told me something about driving like mad and being scared to death but I had my mind on the lapels of that coat, thinking how intriguingly different they looked on her.

She took a fresh breath. "And I need a detective. Or they'll find me and kill me. I want to hire you."

"Certainly," I said in a high falsetto. I brought it down an octave or two. "Let's go . . . er . . . to my apartment. It's right across the street. I'll mix a couple of drinks and put on a few old dance records. And you can tell me what's bothering you." I cleared my throat. "I may even tell you what's bothering me . . ."

THREE'S A SHROUD

BY RICHARD S. PRATHER

A FAWCETT GOLD MEDAL BOOK

FAWCETT PUBLICATIONS, INC., GREENWICH, CONN.
MEMBER OF AMERICAN BOOK PUBLISHERS COUNCIL, INC.

CONTENTS

Blood Ballot

THE EVENING started out in a horrible welter of confusion and for a while I didn't know what was coming off. To tell you the truth, I didn't care.

When a luscious, wild-looking, toothsomely-torsoed tomato starts running at you, and when she has very few clothes on indeed, and when this is in a night club on Beverly Boulevard in Hollywood and she is not part of the floor show, you do not stop to wonder what else is coming off. You leap to your feet and open your eyes wide. At least you do if your name is Shell Scott.

It happened soon after I hit the Starlight Room on Beverly, a small club of the type called "intimate." It was six P.M., too early for the dinner crowd, and only about a dozen customers were present. State Senator Paul Hershey, the guy I was supposed to meet here, wasn't one of them, so I got a ringside table, ordered a bourbon and water and waited, wondering what was up.

For two months Paul Hershey had been my client. He was finishing his first two-year term in the California State Legislature, running for re-election in the general elections now only three weeks off, but he had powerful opposition, most of it named Joe Blake. Blake wasn't on the ballot, but his hand-picked candidate was. Blake didn't run for office; he owned a lot of guys who did run, most of whom were elected.

Hershey, a man who took his job seriously, had consistently fought Blake's men in the legislature for two years, and as a result it looked as if his political goose were cooked. There'd been an increasingly vicious campaign against Hershey since he'd got his party's nomination in the primary, complete with smear and innuendo, most of the slimy barrage financed by Joe Blake. Which figured.

Because Blake was about as big a crook as L.A. had yet produced. Knowing it was one thing; proving it was another. Hershey wanted to prove it and put Blake out of circulation not only because that would virtually guarantee

9

his own re-election but because he strongly felt Joe Blake should be in the clink. He was right. So Hershey had hired a private investigator, which was where I'd come in.

Working together we'd come up with quite a bit. The big item consisted of three signed statements citing Blake's bribery of public officials, subornation of perjury, even evidence that he'd profited from local narcotics pushing. One of the statements was from a lovely little Mexican tomato who told us she'd gone with Blake for several weeks and then had been unceremoniously dropped by him four months ago—and you have never seen a "woman scorned" until you've seen a peppery little black-eyed Mexican doll who has been unceremoniously dropped. Even after four months she'd sizzled like frying tortillas while giving us her info.

The two other statements were from local hoods who'd been associated for a time with the big man. All three statements, plus other information we'd gathered, were at Hershey's home, but some supporting documents and copies of my reports to Hershey were at my hotel, the Spartan, where the desk clerk was holding them for me.

All of it, we thought, and hoped, was enough to present to a grand jury with a good chance of getting an indictment voted. Hershey and I had been careful to keep our investigation quiet, because crossing Joe Blake was usually Russian roulette with no empty chambers and you first, but we'd always known there was the chance of a leak. And twenty minutes ago Hershey had phoned me and said we were in trouble, and asked me to meet him here.

Halfway through my highball I glanced at the front door as it opened and a blonde babe wearing a strapless tan dress came inside. All I noticed about the guy behind her was that he was tall, because the woman demanded all a man's attention. She was in her middle twenties, maybe five-four, and shaped to drive women into hysterics.

I snatched a fast peek at her face when she gyrated past my table, and saw arched brows over soft eyes, red lips parted over sparkling white teeth, and the clear skin of face and neck and bare shoulders whiter than sea foam in sunlight. But soon, of course, I was looking elsewhere. The jersey dress swept down smoothly over the elsewhere.

She walked, with the tall guy still following her, natural-ly, across the dance floor and paused beside a small table

as the headwaiter bent over and swept the "Reserved" sign
away with a flourish like a matador doing a veronica. Had
he really been a matador, however, and she a bull, he
would have been gored in the chops for sure. I noted half
a dozen other male heads turned to stare at the blonde,
and at least twelve male eyes opened wide, and you would
have thought every guy in this joint was named Shell Scott.

I waved at a waiter, drained my drink and ordered another. And then I noticed that the tall guy was Paul Hershey. This was trouble? Either he'd been so preoccupied
with the blonde that he hadn't seen me, which was possible, or else he'd purposely refrained from stopping at my
table. I stayed in my seat and tried to catch his eye. Catch
his eye; that was a laugh.

The Starlight Room has a four-piece combo that plays
nightly, and I heard a few toots and trills on my right
where the musicians were in place and ready to play. As
they swung into their theme, "Stardust," the waiter re-
turned with my drink. At the same moment the blonde
grabbed Hershey's hand and hauled him onto the dance
floor. They started dancing and after eight bars I was ready
to pour the highball, ice cubes and all, over my head.

The blonde wasn't dancing, she was surrendering; it was
seduction to "Stardust," a five-foot-four-inch caress. She
was molded to Paul like soft plastic. Paul's eyes fell on me
with no recognition in them whatsoever. Then they apparently focused and he half-grinned and opened his mouth
as if to say "Hi!" But his expression changed and I had
a hunch his eyes were glazing.

I finished my drink, and just as if they knew what I was
thinking the combo swung into a rumba. At that most cru-
cial moment a pair of big shoulders blocked my view of all
that movement. I knew what must be going on out there,
but I wanted to *see* it, and I was just about to tell the guy
to move or drop dead when I noticed how big those shoulders were.

The man was medium height, legs and hips normal, but
the size of his chest and disturbingly wide shoulders made
him look deformed. He was five or six feet from me and I
could see only his back, but that was enough. The guy was
Ed Garr, ex-pug, ex-stevedore, ex-con, and according to
many reports, ex-human. He was a tough, dirty, stupid
monster employed as gun and right arm—of Joe Blake.

2. A SMALL electric tingle brushed hairs on the back of my neck. Not that I was afraid of Super Chief, either. But Garr was not the type who frequented "intimate" clubs. If he bathed it must have been infrequently and by accident. I could smell him. I could see the ring of dirt on the back of his neck, the soiled collar of his wilted sports shirt. Coincidence, I told myself; he's just here for a shot of straight gin, he likes music, he's lost. But I didn't believe it.

He was standing very still, shoulders hunched slightly forward as he stared out at the dance floor. He was blocking my view, but I didn't ask him to move. Aside from his not being bright, he wasn't completely sane, and it was impossible to predict his reactions. If I asked him to move, he might; or he might move me, depending on what the pixies told him.

Garr wiggled his shoulders, turned to the side a little, a big dismal-looking hunk of ape-like man with a face like a Quasimodo who'd just been clunked on the head by his bell. His mouth was open and his big floppy lips hung down unglamorously from stained teeth. He seemed worked up, angry about something. His mouth closed. His brow pulled down and his jaw muscles bulged out. He looked back at the dancers and I could see his jaw muscles wiggling; then he walked to his right along the edge of the dance floor and stopped, as if undecided about just where he was going. He looked at the dance floor again.

So did I, and decided that maybe Garr hadn't been angry after all; maybe that dance was what he'd been seeing, and his jaw muscles had been bulging in passion. The blonde would give anybody bulges, and the combo was now in the stretch on that rumba. So was she.

That did it. Here was a woman I wanted to dance with. I'm crazy about dancing anyway, and I was wondering how I'd go about asking her, and even what I should ask for, since "May I have the next dance?" wouldn't describe what she was doing, but something else came up suddenly.

I didn't see Garr walking across the dance floor, didn't see him until he grabbed Paul Hershey's tie in his big right hand. His fist couldn't have moved more than six inches, because he never let go of the tie, but he clipped Hershey on the chin and let him dangle at the tie's end for a moment, then dropped him and swung toward the blonde.

She stood straight and still, shocked into immobility, one hand pressed against each side of her white face and her mouth open, lips pulled back. Garr wrapped his hand in the cloth of her dress and jerked it down, ripping it. The music stopped. The room was completely silent.

In that silence she stood motionless, frozen into a kind of sculptured marble, hands still pressed against her face. Garr stared at her, mumbling, big chest heaving; Hershey lay sprawled at their feet. I got out of my chair and started forward just as the blonde moved.

The door was behind me and she started running out the same way she'd come in, straight toward me. Her face was twisted, lips stretched against her teeth, and she was making choking sounds in her throat. I don't think she even saw me. She banged right into me, forcing me back a step, and I could see the pain and anger and embarrassment on her face.

Hardly thinking about what I was doing, I jerked off my coat and tossed it over her shoulders. Still making those choking sounds she grabbed the coat with one hand and slapped me with the other. She slapped me so hard that my ears were still ringing when I looked around and saw her going out the door onto Beverly Boulevard.

Even under these not exactly normal circumstances, and even after being repaid for my aid with a sock in the chops, she was a lovely sight to see. I'm six-two and a shade over two hundred pounds so my coat covered the vital areas, which on that gal were really vital, but it was eight to five that many pedestrians outside there on Beverly were crying out hoarsely.

There was a loud crash behind me and I jerked around to see Garr leaving the dance floor and heading for the swinging doors leading into the kitchen. A table he'd banged into or flipped over rolled on the floor and the crash still echoed in the Starlight Room, incongruous and completely out of place here, like a burp between sweet nothings. I ran toward the kitchen, hit the swinging doors and skidded to a stop inside.

A fat cook with his white chef's cap on awry was pressed back against a wall, looking toward an open door leading to an alley in the rear. A shiny metal bowl and green hunks of lettuce were spilled on the floor. Another door was open on my left.

I pointed toward the alley. "He go outside?"

"Hell, yes."

I ran out behind the club as tires shrieked and a car motor roared. A light blue Packard sedan raced to the alley's end, across the street and on down the alley, turning left a block farther on.

I went back inside the club. The four-piece combo was trying to liven things up with another rumba, but it sounded like half of them were still playing "Stardust." Paul Hershey wasn't in sight.

Nobody was dancing. Two waiters and several customers stared at me. Or rather at my chest. I looked down. My shoulder harness and the butt of my .38 Colt Special were startling against the white of my shirt. At least I still had my gun. It seemed a good thing; I might be needing it.

3.
HERSHEY groaned and his eyelids fluttered. We were alone in the manager's office and I sat on the edge of a straight-backed chair next to the couch he was on.

He opened his eyes wide, groaned, and asked the almost inevitable question. "What . . . happened?"

"Ed Garr. He hung one on your chin."

Paul shuddered. "Feels like one's still hanging there." He closed his eyes; in about a minute he opened them again and peered around. Then he squinted at me and a look of utter disgust grew on his pleasantly bony face. "Well, Scott," he said, "I see you are out chasing down criminals as usual, shooting Ed Garr, protecting—"

"Wait a minute, Paul." I grinned at him. "Everything happened pretty fast, and that babe wasn't a great help to straight thinking."

"What babe?"

"That tomato you were dancing with." I filled him in on what had happened after he lost interest, then asked, "Who was the gal? And where does Ed Garr fit in?"

Hershey was sitting up on the couch, gently rubbing his bruised chin. He was about an inch shorter than I and thin, the bones of his face prominent but not unpleasantly so. He was in his early forties and not handsome by any means, but TV wouldn't hurt his campaign. He moved his hand and ran it through thick, slightly wavy hair starting to gray.

"The gal was Lorry Weston," he said. "She was about as close as she could get to Blake until a week or two back."

"That would have been close."

He nodded. "And that's where Garr fits in. I guess."

He'd never seen the girl until about an hour ago. Earlier today she'd phoned him, said that one of Blake's men had told her about getting some stuff for Blake that would "ruin Hershey." That was about all she could tell, but it was enough to make Hershey immediately check the safe in his guest room, the safe where he'd kept our "Blake file."

"Not only was it gone," he said, "the whole damned safe was gone."

I stood up. Well, I knew what the trouble was now.

Paul went on, "I had my other important papers in there, too. A lot of private stuff I wouldn't want out. And that letter from Internal Revenue, for one thing."

"The hell with . . ." I stopped, understanding what he meant. Paul had recently received from the tax boys a letter saying some deductions he'd claimed on his last income tax return weren't being allowed. It was an honest mistake, followed by an adverse interpretation of one of about a million tax laws, but the amount Paul owed was several hundred dollars. Ordinarily it would have been routine, but in Blake's hands that letter was good smear material; there wasn't much doubt what he'd do with it.

Paul swore quietly. "In a couple of days I'll be a tax-dodging miser chuckling over money I stole from the voters. You know as well as I do how Blake works."

"Yeah. But Blake's boy isn't elected yet—"

"The hell with that. Those three statements were signed, remember."

"Oh." I hadn't thought of that yet. Those statements were signed not only by Hershey and me but by the people who'd given us the info.

Paul said slowly, "If Blake didn't know for sure what we were up to before this, he sure as hell does now. And he knows the names of three people who spilled to us about him."

"We'd better check. Make sure they're . . . all right."

"I've tried. Phoned them, couldn't reach any of them."

Two of the statements had been from hoods named Andy Nelson and Willie Fein, but I thought of Martita first. Not only because we'd got her statement most recently, three days ago, but because she was Martita. Martita Delgado, the little Mexican gal, with soft black hair and lips redder than hell.

I said slowly, "You don't suppose Blake . . ." The manager's phone was on his desk; I grabbed it, dialed Martita's number in the Parker Hotel, let it ring a dozen times before I hung up. I called Willie Fein and drew another blank, then dialed Andy Nelson's number.

Nelson, the most nervous and jumpy of the three, had changed his address two or three times since giving us his info, keeping us informed but scared half to death that something would go wrong. The main reason he'd spilled was because I'd learned he'd violated parole and put the screws to him. He was a two-time loser.

Nelson was home. When I told him Blake knew by now that he'd spilled to us, he started swearing viciously.

"Slow down," I told him. "I'm sorry, but it's done. Go to City Hall and see Samson, Captain of Homicide. He's a friend of mine and I'll phone him, tell him the score. He'll see that you get someplace to hide out, protection if you want it."

Nelson said he damn well wanted it and hung up with a bang that hurt my ear. I wanted him to get protection too, just in case. No investigator can afford to let his informants get hurt because of info they give him; he runs out of information, and informants, in a hurry that way.

I turned to Hershey. "Nelson's okay. So the others probably are too. For a minute I thought—but Blake's got little to worry about now."

Hershey nodded but didn't say anything, face even longer than usual. I felt no jollier than he did. Joe Blake and I hadn't ever banged really head-on before, but over the years I'd sent two of his boys to Quentin and, recently, one to a cemetery. Consequently, on the one occasion when we'd met, he'd told me politely to keep my nose out of his business or get used to a nose with rigor mortis. It's well known that you can't get rigor mortis in just your nose.

I said, "You got any idea when the safe was lifted?"

"Last night some time but I don't know when. Merchant's Union asked me to speak last night. I was at the dinner from about six last night till almost two this morning, had a few drinks after I talked to them—" he smiled slightly—"and told them why they should vote for me."

"Merchant's Union? Seems like Blake's men run the thing. That's what I heard; funny they'd ask you in for a political speech. Did this Lorry Weston tell you who tipped her?" He shook his head. "Screwy thing. She spills, you bring her here—then Ed Garr shows up, pops you and yanks her dress half off. I know he isn't the most brilliant personality in L.A., but this is a quaint one even for him."

"You know as much now as I do."

"She say *why* she tipped you off?"

"No. I called her back this afternoon before I phoned you, arranged for us to have dinner here. She drove down and met me right outside. Thought we might find out what the score was." He shook his head. "Didn't even get a chance to talk with her any more, though. She didn't act as if she wanted to talk, anyway. I kept telling her and telling her we'd better get down to business. But you'd think she was deaf or something."

"Or something. Maybe she's in a different business." I grinned at him, then sobered. "Think she might have been some kind of plant? After all, Garr showed up right behind her."

"I don't know, never thought about it." He wiggled his jaw gently. "Let's get out of here. Maybe we can think of something at my place."

"Meet you there."

In the Cad I unstrapped my too-obvious holster, shoved it under the seat, then U-turned and headed down Beverly. My route took me within a couple blocks of the Parker Hotel so I stopped there. Room 27 was empty; the desk clerk told me that Miss Delgado had checked out last night at seven P.M. Two men had come to see her and she'd gone away with them. No, she'd left no forwarding address.

I looked the room over, but there was nothing in it, except maybe memory of the first time I'd seen little Martita here. I'd got a tip from one of my informants, who'd been keeping an ear open for me, that this Delgado girl was an ex-flame of Blake's and could probably tell me plenty. I'd located her in the Parker and convinced her— for three hundred bucks—that she should tell Hershey and me her tale, which she'd done.

But when I'd knocked that first time and she'd answered

the door, Martita had been enough to make me forget what I'd come to see her about. At least temporarily. She'd been wearing a blue robe, about as thick and opaque as cellophane, brushing long black hair that was spread out in a shining mass over her shoulders. We'd talked a little while and I'd told her what I was after, and finally she'd said sure, she'd be glad to cooperate any way at all.

But the room was empty now, and there was no way to know where she'd gone, or why. Walking down to the Cad I kept thinking of her softness, the devil in her big dark eyes.

4.

HERSHEY had a couple of drinks mixed by the time I reached his house. He showed me where the guest room window had been jimmied, pointed out a deep indentation in the grass outside, undoubtedly where the safe had been shoved through the window before being carted away. Back in the front room Hershey sat on the edge of a chair while I used his phone to call City Hall and got Homicide. Captain Samson answered.

"Sam? Shell here." Since Sam is about my best friend in L.A., he knew all about the job Hershey and I had been doing. I briefed him on the latest revolting development and told him that Andy Nelson, the only one of our three informants I'd located, was on his way down, shaking visibly.

"That'll make two," he said. "We got another one down here."

"What do you mean, Sam?" I didn't like the sound of his voice. *"Who* do you mean?"

"Couple of the boys found the body in an alley about midnight last night. It was Willie Fein. He's in the morgue now. Three forty-five slugs in his chest."

"He's dead?"

"Of course not, he's in the morgue for a transfusion. Three forty-five slugs—"

"Okay, Sam, knock it off. I believe you."

Hershey asked me what was the matter.

"They got Willie," I said. "Killed him last night."

Paul winced, shook his head slowly.

"Sam," I said into the phone, "this might be important. Was he worked over first?"

"Plenty. Somebody beat the bejeezus out of him." He was quiet a moment, then added, "Something else you might want to play with. Pretty near the same time, Highway Patrol found another guy in a ditch with three forty-fives in his ticker—and before you ask, he was dead too."

"Any connection?"

"Don't know if there is, but the guy worked for Joe Blake. Young punk, name of Stu Robb. Mean anything to you?"

"No, it doesn't," I said slowly, "not yet, anyway." Sam hadn't heard anything from or about Martita Delgado. I thanked him and hung up.

"They killed him," Hershey said softly. "Murdered him."

He sounded, and looked, sick. He stood up and walked forward a couple steps, stopped and said hesitantly, "I never really thought they'd . . . I guess I shouldn't have started this. It wouldn't have happened." He looked bewildered.

"Come off it, Paul. You'll have me thinking you popped the guy yourself." He winced again, but he lost the bewildered look. "Blake had him killed," I went on, "and Blake is the only reason he's dead; just because we dug up some dirt, and got part of it from Willie, doesn't change that. Willie was long overdue anyway."

He was quiet for a while. Then he frowned and said, "How did they find out we had the stuff? Or that it was here?"

"Looks like they got to Willie somehow, beat the truth out of him, then searched here. Willie wouldn't have known about the other affidavits, but we took all three here in the house. When Blake's boys got the affidavits with the names on them they probably took off to pick up the other two, Martita and Nelson, only Nelson had moved." I paused. "And they killed Willie."

Hershey sat down again. "It's incredible. Can you imagine a man like Blake controlling men in the legislature, backing candidates who—"

I cut him off. "Yeah, I can imagine it. Look, those affidavits gave him our names too. They searched here; might be they gave my place a once-over. I'd better check."

I got up. "And don't look so glum, Paul. They can't have found the stuff at my hotel desk, so we've got that. There's still Nelson and you and me. Probably Martita too. We can do the damn statements over again, except for Willie's."

That didn't cheer him up much. When I left he was grim, still looking a little sick. I didn't feel so good myself. But I pushed thoughts of Willie Fein, who now had rigor mortis in his nose, out of my mind and climbed into the Cad. Under the right circumstances I wanted to see Blake; even Ed Garr. I rather hoped I'd see Lorry Weston again, too. She still had my coat.

I didn't get the car out of second gear. Half a block from Hershey's was a stop sign. A guy leaned against it smoking a cigarette, but most of my attention was on a car that had pulled out from the curb right after me. As I stopped at the intersection the other car swung up fast on my left —and the Cad's right-hand door opened. I didn't even have time to grab under the seat for my gun.

A big .45 automatic came inside followed by a young punk with thin brown hair and a permanent sneer stuck on his white, weak-looking face. I'd seen his mugg shots at headquarters. Dee Tolman, and I knew all about him, including the fact that he was another soldier in Blake's army.

He said in a high, girlish voice that went with his delicate features but not with his personality, "Hands on the wheel, Dad. Don't get excited."

The other car was slanted in front of my left fender and I heard one of its doors slam; the Cad's door on my side opened and a guy fanned me for a gun and grunted. I could smell him. These were not the right circumstances, but it was Ed Garr.

"No heater." His voice rumbled softly in my ear.

"No heater."

He shoved me roughly past the middle of the seat and got under the wheel. His shoulder mashed me against Dee Tolman and I could feel the .45's muzzle, knew where it was if I wanted to grab for it. I didn't want to. I could see two men in the other buggy. The gun in my side also helped discourage me. And then there was Garr.

He put the Cad in gear and I said, "Where we headed, Garr?"

"See Joe."

That was all of the conversation. The other car fell in behind us.

5.   JOE BLAKE lived only four or five miles from the Hollywood business district, but his two-story brick home was at the end of half a mile of narrow dirt road lined with eucalyptus trees, the road being the only way in or out. There wasn't another house for a mile, just a lot of trees in rock and boulder-filled ground. The isolation was some protection against guys who might not like Joe Blake, of whom there were plenty, but it was an open secret because Blake wanted it open, figuring it made even more sense to discourage people that way than having alarms go off in their ears. It was my guess that he also had everything from radar to tommy guns out here, and I knew several of his tough boys were always handy. Joe Blake didn't trust people.

At the road's end a gravel drive curved in front of the house, continued on around in an oval to join the road again. Grass filled the oval, and cement steps led up to the front door. Parked near the steps was a maroon Lincoln I recognized as Blake's.

A big ugly character opened the door, looked at us, then turned and walked ahead to the end of a short hallway. The leather loop of a sap dangled from his hip pocket. He unlocked a door at the hall's end, let us through into another hallway running left and right, locked the door again behind us. No open house here.

Joe Blake was waiting for us in one of the bedrooms, wearing a terry cloth robe and leather slippers. A big briar pipe was stuck in his mouth. He looked a bit Hollywoodish, but it wasn't a pose. Blake liked to be comfortable, and he liked to smoke a briar pipe, and he usually did what he liked to do. If he felt like having a guy shoot you, say, he told the guy, "Shoot him." He wore horn-rimmed glasses and didn't look like a man who controlled much of California politics and crime. Who does? Blake was about five-ten, forty-six years old, slender, and not bad-looking, except that he looked meaner than hell. Of course, he was meaner than hell.

He grinned at me and said, "Hi. Have a chair, Mr. Scott." He pointed, and sat on the edge of his bed. "Good to see you. Glad you came."

"I got your invitation." I sat down.

He laughed, pushed his glasses up a little with his thumb. "The boys are good at delivering invitations."

"They gave a beaut to Willie Fein."

He laughed some more. Pretty soon somebody would come in with tea and cookies. "Who's Willie Fein?"

This time we laughed together. It was warm and friendly here. And the way this crumb was acting I began thinking maybe he'd actually brought me out to kill me. But he could have told his boys to take a stab at it earlier if that was what he'd been after.

I said, "Okay, I'm here. What do you want?"

"Lorry Weston, for one thing," he said. "I'd like to know where she is."

I said truthfully, "So would I. But I don't know."

"You might as well tell me now if you do. There are several ways to make people talk."

"The answer would still be the same. You can't get blood out of . . ." I stopped, because the cliché wasn't sparkling conversation and I am no turnip anyway. Garr stared at me, long arms hanging loosely at his sides and his mouth half open; Dee Tolman leaned against the door, the .45 in his hand.

I said to Blake, "Look, I can't jump you and your boys, eat all the guns and bang your heads together. But you can hardly work me over, either—or whatever you've got in mind—and expect to get away with it. Not even you, Blake. That would make a bigger stink in Los Angeles than Ed Garr does. So let's quit playing around."

"All right, Scott. I'll lay it out." He leaned back on two pillows at the top of the bed, laced his hands behind his head and said casually, "We aren't fooling each other a bit anyway. I know you and Hershey have been after my neck for quite a while—" he smiled gently—"and never mind how I know."

"Wouldn't have anything to do with Willie Fein."

He grinned. "Who's Willie Fein? You and Hershey got little stories from three people; you don't have them any more. But you two, with Nelson, might get together with a cop or a grand jury and embarrass me a little. Follow me? You couldn't hurt me, but it wouldn't be good this close to election."

He paused for a moment. I knew why he hadn't included Willie Fein. Willie wouldn't be talking to anybody any more. But I wondered why he'd left out Martita Delgado.

"So," Blake continued, "I'd like for you to drop out."

"What do you mean, drop out?"

"Just that. Drop Hershey. Give me your word that you won't help him another minute, won't spill any testimony against me or my boys—in other words climb clear out of my hair."

I started to interrupt, but he raised his voice and went on, "You see, Scott, without your help, Hershey's dead." He laughed. "I mean in the election—I can't touch him physically; too well known that I'm out for his scalp. But without your testimony, your help, the screws you've got in Andy—I know Nelson's in the damper, but I can get to him there—the weight you can swing, I haven't got a thing to worry about. Clear?"

"Sure it's clear. And maybe you're right. Only I wouldn't help you cut your throat." I wasn't going to give this bum my word on anything. At least not for the first half-hour or so of the beating. Besides which I wasn't simply going to lie down and say, "Hit me, boys." Dee was wiggling his gun gently, as if he enjoyed the feel of it, or were anticipating my lack of enjoyment at the feel of it.

Blake said, "One other thing. I could tell by looking over the stuff I got that there was more somewhere. You must have it—not in your apartment or office, though."

"If some of your goons ripped up—"

"Neat as a pin," he interrupted. "Boys looked around, but you won't be able to tell they did. I'd like the rest of the stuff, Scott."

I didn't say anything. It was his party.

"I know what you're thinking," he said pleasantly. "You're not going to give this crumb Blake the back of your hand, right? But you're not a complete fool, Scott. I'll get what I want one way or another. If you cooperate, we settle this and nobody gets hurt. Not you, not Hershey, not anybody. You keep playing tough-boy and it'll just be a mess all around. And I'll still get what I'm after."

"Forget it, Blake."

"Would you cooperate to keep somebody from a very bad time?"

"Like what?"

"Like having some teeth knocked out, and developing a few internal injuries. And—" he gave me that gentle smile again—"dying."

He's talking about me, I thought dismally. "Blake, you

may be clear out of your mind, but Robb and Willie are
already in the morgue. You scatter any more corpses
around, and people are going to start talking about you.
The election will be the least of your worries." I stood up.
"And just one little thing I hadn't mentioned. You or your
boys lay one finger on me here and now, and somebody *else*
is going to get killed here and now."

He chuckled and got off the bed, walked past me to the
door. "Come on."

He went out. Dee pointed his gun at me, a smile on his
girlish face. I followed Blake from the room, halfway down
the hall, and stopped beside him at another door. He stuck
a key in the lock and shoved the door open, then said,
"Look in there, Scott. I wasn't talking about you."

Then I saw her. He'd been talking about Martita Delgado.

6. SHE LAY on her back on a bed at the far side
of the room, hands bound beneath her, a
white gag over her mouth. A reddish-purple
bruise was ugly on her left cheek. She was fully clothed,
even to high heels and nylon stockings, but her white
blouse had been torn. Her eyes were closed, but as I walked
toward her she raised her head slightly and her lids parted.
Then her eyes opened wide and automatically she started
to speak, the gag muffling her voice. The black eyes seemed
enormous.

Blake put a hand on my arm as I stepped toward her.

"You filthy—" I said.

It bounced right off him, but he stepped back out of
reach, and it was just as well that he did. For both of us.
Garr stood inside the room, Dee behind him.

Blake said, "I don't have to spell it out for a smart guy
like you, do I?" His voice had changed, and it wasn't just
the sarcasm in his tone. It was tighter, less pleasant. "The
boys here could pound on you a while, but if we let you go
you might keep on giving me trouble. And, frankly, if they
polished you off and dumped you somewhere, there might
be a little noise. There's fifty other guys in town with good
reason to knock you off, Scott, but it wouldn't look too
good for me—although I can get away with it if you make
me. But this way I figure you'll cooperate."

"Go to hell."

He shrugged. "You know what happens to her if you don't play along with me. Oh, we'll get a little amusement out of her before we kill her."

I stared at him, and my revulsion and disgust must have showed in my face. He laughed softly and went on, "Yes, she's very amusing."

"Shut up, Blake." I had spoken so softly that at first I wasn't sure he'd heard me. But he stopped talking, licked his lips and glanced toward the door. "I wonder how wise you'd be," I said, "or how tough, if those two guns weren't right behind you."

That was the first thing I'd said that ruffled his composure. His face got harder, cold. But in a moment his expression smoothed. "It should be clear, Scott. Just agree to what I said and she'll be okay—and so will you. That last is something we haven't talked about."

"Yeah, just agree, and Martita and I walk out of here hand in hand."

"Not quite like that. Not that I think you'd cross me once you make up your mind to go along, but I'll have to keep her here for a while—till the elections. Just to make sure you stay in line."

I looked at Martita. Her eyes were fixed on my face. Blake said, "No matter what you decide, you walk out anyway."

"Sure."

He explained, "I mean, you can leave right now if you feel like it. I wanted to show you this—" he nodded toward the bed—"and let you know what I expect. You've got the picture now. Take it or leave it."

I didn't say anything. On the bed, Martita made muffled noises.

Blake said, "The boys aren't even going to work you over. I told you why, but I didn't think any argument would be needed. I thought you were a regular good Samaritan, sort of an unchaste Galahad. So they tell me, sucker."

He'd used the right word. It is well and widely known that I'm a sucker for a damsel in distress. She doesn't even have to be in distress.

"Maybe I was wrong," Blake said. "Think it over."

I swallowed. "I don't have to think it over. No deals, Blake. I won't make any deals with you."

I wanted to get my hands on him, squeeze his neck a little. Dee was in the room, though, and the .45 was pointed unwaveringly at my chest. I'd play hell making any fast moves. A .45 slug, just in my hand, would toss me halfway across the room. So, for that matter, might Garr. He stared stupidly at me from dull eyes, his droopy lips hanging down as usual.

Blake shrugged again, looking disappointed. "Okay," he said. "All right, Ed."

Garr smiled loosely. In that soft, rumbling voice of his he said, "You mean now, Joe?"

Blake nodded and Garr's smile widened. He walked toward the bed, passing within a yard of me. The stink of him filled my nostrils. Martita was making whimpering sounds behind the gag, squirming on the bed, pushing with her heels. As Garr got close to her she drew her legs up and thrust them forward convulsively, pushed herself completely off the bed and onto the floor.

"What the hell is this, Blake?"

He looked at me. "I didn't want to ruin the merchandise till you got here, Scott. I'm a fair, reasonable man, and I wanted to be fair about this. So far she's got a couple bruises, but she hasn't been hurt at all any other way. Garr's been mighty anxious, though. Not often he gets a chance like—but you say no deal, so there isn't any point in holding him back any longer."

Garr bent over and picked Martita up in his two big paws as if she were a doll, effortlessly, dropped her onto the bed. She squirmed away, making those whimpering sounds in her throat, but he mashed his left hand against her.

My heart was pounding. "Blake," I said, "you must be clear out of your mind. Garr's crazy. He's really crazy, not sane. Stop him."

He grinned, looked back at the bed. Garr was still holding Martita with his left hand, looking down at her. She kicked at him but he held her easily. Finally Martita stopped kicking futilely, lay still, not whimpering. Garr stared at her.

"I tell you, he's nuts," I said. "He might . . . might kill her." Blake laughed at that. "In the Starlight," I said rapidly. "He hit Hershey, right there in the club, jerked Lorry's dress half off. There's no telling—"

"I know all about that," Blake said. "Ed told me he'd

been a bad boy." He chuckled. "That's how it happened I sent for you. Ed's, oh, impulsive at times, makes a few mistakes. But he's loyal, a good man. Man deserves a reward of some kind, little bonus once in a while."

Garr's face was flushed. For a moment I forgot that Blake and Tolman were even in the room, just saw Ed Garr, a filthy ape. And I started toward him.

I started, but that was all. At my first step Dee Tolman said sharply, "Go ahead." I took one more step and stopped, muscles in my back tightening. Garr had turned to look at me, but Martita lay quietly, head turned to the left and her eyes squeezed tight.

"Change your mind?" Blake asked.

"No."

"Let's get out of here then." He chuckled again.

I turned as Dee stepped away from the door. Blake went out. After a moment I followed him. As Dee started to shut the door I got a glimpse of the bed, Martita lying very still and Garr standing, bent over her. The door closed.

7.

WE WENT into Blake's bedroom again, Dee careful not to get near me, careful to keep the automatic on me all the time. Inside, Blake sprawled on the bed. I said, "For Christ's sake, you can't be serious. You aren't going to—"

"Oh, shut up, Scott. And what's there to get so excited about? She's no babe in arms."

I sat down, then got up again. I couldn't sit still.

Blake said, "I wonder if he'll take that gag off her. If she yells, that's all it'll mean. He won't hurt her."

I knew what he meant. We'd left her and Garr only a minute ago or a little more, but my face was wet with perspiration, my shirt was damp.

Blake said, "If it bothers you, beat it. I said you could blow."

I turned toward the door, then stopped. I could feel my fists clench and unclench, and I said without looking at Blake, "All right, get that punk out of there."

I heard him swing his heels to the floor and turned to look at him as he said, "You'll go along?"

"Yes."

"It's a deal then? You lay off?"

"Just the way you spelled it out. If you're leveling with me, no strings."

"I'm leveling."

"It's a deal," I said. "Get him out of there."

I was hoping Blake would send Dee, Dee and his gun, in which case there would have been a much mangled Blake in ten seconds. But Blake went himself. First, though, he said, "Where's the rest of the stuff? I know you've got it."

"My hotel. Desk. You'll get it."

He went out. It seemed to take a hell of a time, but it probably was only half a minute or so. Then Blake came inside with Garr, who looked like a big overgrown sulking boy. A boy punk. I called him that. I called Blake and Dee several things, too. They let me run down, then had me write a note to Jimmy, clerk at the Spartan desk, telling him to give the envelope to the bearer. Garr went for it.

Blake was pleased, grinning. He said to me, "You came through just in time, just barely. Another fifteen seconds even—but I figured you would, Scott." He shook his head. "Well, I'll keep my end of the deal, but I still say you're a sucker. How you can get all worked up over a little girl like that Mex babe—"

"Let me see her."

"You go—" He cut it off, shrugged and said, "Might as well."

She was in almost the same position as when I'd first seen her here. Her left cheek was pressed into the pillow and her black eyes were sober, fixed on me as I stopped beside the bed.

"I'd like to talk to her," I said.

Blake didn't answer me for a moment, then he walked to the other side of the bed and leaned toward Martita. "Listen to me. You let out any more yells and I'll shut your mouth good this time." He paused. "Or let Ed do it."

He took off the gag. She pressed her lips together, moistened them, and I leaned forward with my hand against the pillow. "You okay, Martita?"

She nodded but didn't speak for several seconds. Then she said, "I thought you'd gone. I can't tell you . . . Shell, thank you. Thank—"

"Forget it." I was griped, griped at everything.

Martita moved her head forward slightly and pressed

her lips against the back of my hand. Blake roughly fixed the gag over her mouth again. I could still feel the softness of her lips on my skin.

We went out. When Garr came back with the envelope Blake checked its contents, then raised an eyebrow at me. "How'd you find out I bought off Judge Lewis?"

"I guessed it. You slimy—"

"Beat it. You want Dee to give you a little push with that popgun of his? And stay the hell away from me. From now on. Be a good idea if you beat it clear out of town."

I told him what he could do with that. "You've got your deal. But that's all you've got."

"I've still got the girl. Beat it."

"She'll be all right?"

"She'll be okay. You've got my word."

I said a foul word of my own. "She'd better be okay."

"She will be, as long as you don't cross me. I'll turn her loose election day. And by the way, Scott, don't go to your buddy-buddy Samson or anybody else. If you do, you'll never find her. Not alive. And I'll be covered eight ways from the middle. Now beat it."

My throat was tight. I stared at him a minute, then turned and walked out. Nobody stopped me. The ugly guard unlocked the front door and smirked at me. I hit him on the chin and he reeled back against the wall, slumped to the carpet. I went to the Cad and felt under the seat for my .38. It was still there. I strapped on the holster, held the gun in my hand for a long minute, looking back toward the hcuse. Then I drove slowly down the narrow road, toward Hollywood, wondering what I'd say to Paul Hershey.

8.

I PARKED in front of the Spartan Apartment Hotel, got out and walked toward the entrance. Behind me somebody called, "Mr. Scott?"

I swung around as my name was called again, the sound coming from across the street. My hotel is on the opposite side of North Rossmore from the Wilshire Country Club and I couldn't see who was in the shadows over there. But it was a woman's voice. I grabbed my gun, though, and held it before me as I walked toward the shadows.

And then I saw the faint gleam of light on white, white legs curving deliciously down from a man's coat. My coat.

Her two hands held the coat together in front. And above it was the gleam of long blonde hair, the blur of a lovely face.

"Well, *hello!*" I said.

She reached for my hand and accidentally grabbed the gun and let out a squeal and let go of the coat and I almost emptied my gun into the air whooping like an Indian. My eyes were getting accustomed to the gloom.

I stuck the gun back into its holster and she reached for my hand again, this time using only one hand of her own, and said rapidly, "I'm about to die. I've been here so long. Oh! You *are* Sheldon Scott, aren't you?"

"Shell, call me Shell. That's me. Well, this is . . . a pleasant surprise. How in hell do you happen to be out here?"

In a fast rush of words she told me that Hershey had mentioned my name to her at the Starlight—probably between gasps, I imagined—and after she'd run out of there she'd got into her car and driven clear out of town. "I drove and drove, just *mad,*" she said, "and then I parked. I couldn't go back to the hotel—if Ed found me, Ed Garr —he'd kill me, I knew. Then I looked through the coat, your wallet was in it and I saw your card and address, that you're a detective, the one Paul mentioned." She stopped, took a deep breath. "And I need you."

She, with her eyes completely accustomed to the gloom, must have seen the flash of my teeth. "You do? Well, Miss Weston—or Lorry? Lorry, I, too—"

"I need a detective. I'll have to explain to you—I never did get to tell Paul—but I'm afraid Garr or Joe will find me. They'll kill me. I want to hire you."

"You have."

"Oh, good. Mr. Scott, I don't know. . . . Listen, do we have to just stand here?"

"No, certainly not. I'm sorry. Let's go . . . to my apartment. It's right across the street. That's it, I'll mix a couple drinks and put on a few old dance records. And you can tell me what's bothering you. I may even tell you what's bothering me."

I might have told her then, but she took my arm and we walked across the street, into the Spartan lobby and up to the desk. Jimmy mentioned the manila envelope and I told him I'd sent for it. He frowned slightly, at Lorry's mannish coat, but she was holding it tightly around her so she just looked like a beautiful eccentric gal in a man's coat. He gave me the key and as we started up the stairs I heard a high wailing sound from Jimmy, who apparently had just noticed the extent of Lorry's eccentricity, and as we reached the first turn in the stairs my next-door neighbor, Dr. Anson, passed us on his way down. Tonight he went down faster than usual.

He gave me a grin and said, "Hi, Shell, what's new . . ." and then as we walked higher there was a thumping and bumping on the stairs below us. It was my guess that there was a dizzy conversation going on between Jimmy and Dr. Anson by the time Lorry and I reached my apartment and I unlocked the door, escorted her inside, and quickly locked the door again.

"How lovely," Lorry said, looking around.

"It's home," I said, not looking around. She walked forward slowly, her back to me.

She stopped and peered at the two tanks of tropical fish inside the door, glanced at Amelia, my garish nude over the fake fireplace, then sat down on the chocolate-brown oversized divan. Oversized means big enough for at least two people, but I pulled a hassock over in front of the divan, sat down facing her and went right to the heart of the problem: "What would you like to drink?"

She said she didn't care, she could use a drink, though, after standing next to that creepy Country Club for so long. I mixed a bourbon-and-water for me, a gin-and-orange juice for her. We sipped the drinks and talked for a few minutes, and I listened mostly, and looked.

Lorry Weston had relaxed and leaned back on the divan, drink in one hand, other hand holding the coat together, and sitting there four feet from me she was a sight to see.

"You've got green eyes, haven't you?" I said.

"What? Oh, yes, they're green. Bluish sometimes, but usually green." She smiled, and it was a smile to raise temperatures, to play hell with spines, then she went on slowly, "I didn't think you could tell from way over there. You're quite observant."

"Oh, yes."

The smile got even broader, and my spine was a fuse ignited from the bottom. Just before it lit my brain I looked determinedly at the ceiling and said, "Go ahead, Lorry."

"Go ahead and what?"

"Ahead with what you were saying."

She'd already told me that until ten days ago she'd been very close to Joe Blake. Close enough to spend quite a bit of time with him, at his house, but not quite close enough to move in with him, which he'd wanted her to do. He was no fool. Their relationship had lasted a couple of months, about par for the course, then Blake had dropped her like a hot tomato, suddenly, being crude about it. Lorry hadn't known in the beginning that Blake was breaking half the laws in the book; when she'd found out she'd started getting leery of him, and the yen she'd had for him at first had begun wearing off even before he'd kicked her out. The way he'd told her to get lost, though, being sarcastic and contemptuous, had been the last straw.

She went on, "It made me simply furious. Even if I didn't mind the break, no woman likes being treated that way. Why, that *never* happened to me before."

"I'll bet not, I'll bet—"

"He's a fiend, I tell you. Something wrong with him, got to have *new* . . . something new all the time. Even when I met him he was going with somebody else and he just kicked her out. A fiend. But the way he treated me made me almost hate him."

Lorry developed the "woman scorned" angle, which seemed to be part of Blake's standard operating procedure, then said, "A couple of the fellows, his staff or whatever he called it, always hung around me while Joe and I were together. They knew he never stuck with one woman very long, and I guess they thought maybe they could . . . pick up the pieces. So I sort of strung one of them along for a week or so. Just to keep in touch with what Joe was up to if I could. That's how I found out they'd stolen something from Paul Hershey."

"Not so fast. Who were these guys?"

"Robbie and Ed Garr."

Garr. And Stu Robb, who'd been dead in that ditch last night. "They stole the stuff from Paul?"

"Yes. Robbie was always after me to go out with him. I did a couple times after Joe and I split, and I let him come up to my place in the Ambassador Hotel last night. That's when he told me they'd got that stuff."

"Wait a second. You mean Robb blabbed all this to you right after he and Garr lifted Hershey's safe?"

"I didn't know if it was a safe or what, only that it would hurt Mr. Hershey. They'd done whatever it was about an hour before Robbie came up to see me—all through working, he said. And he didn't just blab, like you put it. I told you the only reason I let him hang around was in case he might tell me anything I could use to get back at Joe—so I gave Robbie Martinis in champagne glasses. He's almost as big and stupid as Ed Garr, and you'd suppose it would take a couple of gallons to get him smashed. But alcohol affects the brain, and he has so little brain. Anyway, he told me, and then I got rid of him."

"Feed me Martinis and I'd tell you anything. And you'd have one hell of a time getting rid of me. Hey, would you rather have a Martini?"

"This is fine. But you have one if you want." She turned on one of those smiles again. "As far as Robbie's concerned, I just told him I had a headache. Guess what. He left and came back with a bottle of aspirins. Talk about stupid."

"That wasn't stupid. Ed Garr was your other—other admirer?"

"Uh-huh. Always near me when he could manage it. He'd stand around and stare at me with his tongue hanging out like an old blown-out inner tube. All drooly. You know the type."

"Yeah. My type."

"Silly. You're not a type. I wouldn't have anything to do with that Garr, though. Can you imagine kissing him?"

"Frankly, no."

"I mean a woman. No woman would. Ugh. Those big wet sloppy lips. You know, when he's excited and talking, they splash. You've seen him."

"I've smelled him. Have you any idea how come he popped up at the Starlight?"

She shook her head. She was sorry she'd slapped me when I'd given her my coat, she said; she hadn't been thinking straight. I told her I understood. Lorry talked a while longer, interspersing her conversation with those warm smiles. Under different circumstances, some of her information might have been quite helpful.

One item in particular was that during the time she'd been with Blake at his house, she'd often seen him put papers, papers he was very careful about, in a drawer of a steel desk in his den. The way she described it, I felt pretty sure that the envelope I'd just turned over to him, and all the rest of Hershey's papers which hadn't yet been destroyed, would be in there. It wasn't an ordinary drawer, though; behind its steel door was a safe, and the papers were in the safe. Lorry, however, knew the combination. I blinked at that.

"Baby," I said, "no wonder he wants to find you."

"Oh, he doesn't know I've got the combination."

I said slowly, "How come you know something as important to Blake as that? He'd hardly tell you."

"Hardly. Never mind. I know what it is."

It sounded funny. I wondered again if she might be pulling my leg, but discarded that thought. She'd hardly have been a party to that caper in the Starlight. Adding up a lot of "ifs," though—if she were on the level, if Blake and I were not precariously allied, if he didn't have Martita, if Lorry would tell me that combination and I could get in and out of Blake's house without being killed—Hershey and I might get out of our hole while putting Blake into a deep one. And if brains were eggs I'd be thinking with an omelet.

"Lorry," I said, "don't tell me you peeked over Blake's shoulder and saw him twirling dials. A guy as careful as he is? I find it difficult to believe."

She frowned. "That's not a very nice thing to say."

"I knew that when I said it."

She stared at me for several seconds, then said slowly, "It's a new combination. He had a man change it about a week before we split. Nobody knew it except Joe, and he wouldn't write anything like that down. I guess he thought about it a lot so he wouldn't forget." She paused, then said flatly, "Sometimes he talks in his sleep."

"I'm a low, fiendish type, Lorry. But I'll never doubt you again. Tell me anything at all and I'll believe you."

"You're an idiot."

"I believe you."

"You're a nasty old man."

"I'm not old." There was something I'd wanted to find out before, but she'd wriggled carelessly and I'd forgotten.

I said, "About Stu Robb. He ran off at the mouth to you last night, then took off, huh? What time was that?"

"He came up at ten and stayed maybe an hour. Left about eleven, I guess. Why?"

"Honey," I said, "don't you know Robb's dead?"

9.

HER SHOCK could hardly have been faked. "Dead?" she said finally. "What do you mean, he's dead?"

"Just that. Highway Patrol spotted him around midnight. Him and Willie Fein—that's two people dead already. So excuse me if I say some things you don't like."

"I see." She was quiet for a while, then said softly, "Could I have had anything to do—"

"Don't worry about it. You didn't say anything to Hershey until today, anyway. So relax."

That was a laugh. If she got any more relaxed I was going to take a cold shower.

"That's right," she said. "I don't know where Ed Garr came from there at the Starlight, but he's crazy about me, you know. And plain crazy. I guess when he saw me with Paul—of all people—and dancing like that, he must have flipped. He isn't stable."

"He did flip." Lorry didn't sound angry any more. And she had said dancing "like that." So she did know how she danced. I excused myself for a moment, walked to the portable record player I have in the bedroom—and it is none of your business what my record player is doing in the bedroom—switched it on, complete with a couple Stanley Black records. Rumbas!

Then I slyly took off my shoulder harness and that lumpy gun, walked back into the living room in time to a whole mess of drums and people shrieking. As I sat down on my hassock I said, "Pretty, huh? You know, I feel rhythmic as hell."

Her lips were curved into a slight smile, a good sign, and she was gently chewing on the inside of her cheek, her lips moving sensually. Anyway, they were moving, and as far as I was concerned they were moving sensually.

"It's good to be here," she said. "I was so scared. I knew I couldn't go back to the hotel. Couldn't go much of any-place dressed like this." She smiled. "Besides, I wanted to bring back your coat."

For one wild moment I thought maybe she meant to give it to me right then. But she didn't. She said, "I thought you might be willing to help me."

I told her I was more than willing, that she could hide out here for weeks. Even as I said it, though, it occurred to me that my apartment might not be the best spot for her to hide out; not with Blake looking for her. But my mind at this point was not up to grappling with such complicated thinking.

I was looking at Lorry, my brain merely a sponge soaking up sensation. It had happened. I could hear her talking, and somehow I managed to answer her. I was hired, I was to help her, protect her, be her bodyguard, keep Blake and Garr and Company from shooting holes in her.

She said, "I feel *so* much better, Shell. I don't have any money on me—" she laughed throatily—"as I suppose you'd guessed. I understand investigators are usually given a . . . what is it, retainer?"

"In this case we can skip it. You don't even have to pay me." I was clear out of my head.

She chuckled. "How nice. I could kiss you for that. Maybe . . . maybe we could call a kiss the retainer."

"Baby, we could call it the fee."

My voice sounded hoarse. So would your voice have sounded hoarse. Lorry was sitting on the couch facing me, leaning back, relaxed as hell. For a while she'd held my coat together with one hand, but she was doing that no longer. So far the coat had been doing a fairly good job of things. But now all that had changed; it was doing a simply horrible, or completely marvelous, job of things. Depending, of course, upon your point of view.

Somewhere in my mind a small voice was saying, "Look away, look away," but that voice was so very small, and there was another voice, a great big booming voice, crying more interesting things in my head.

I heard some small noises, but supposed it was only blood cells exploding or my discs slipping, and I guess I heard the door open, actually heard it. But it didn't mean anything to me; nothing was going to distract me now. The only thing that could possibly interrupt my reverie would be for somebody to hit me on the head.

And wouldn't you know? Somebody hit me on the head.

10. My first thoughts on awakening were very dim ones, jumbled and not at all clear. I thought: Lorry, what did you *do?* And why? We were getting along famously, weren't we?

All this time I was sprawled on the carpet, but by the time I struggled to my seat I'd remembered other things. Those noises, the sound of the door opening; slowly the rest of my memory came back. Lorry had jerked suddenly away from me and cried out, *"Ed!"*

She'd had time for only one word, and if I'd had time for even one word it would have been a coarse word indeed, but I'd had no time. Anyway, Ed would have been Ed Garr, and he'd hit me on the head. It seemed that history was repeating itself. When Lorry had danced with Hershey, Garr had suddenly arrived and hit *him* on the head.

Could Lorry, I wondered, have gone through all this routine just to set me up for Garr? Could she have been pulling my leg? But I knew I'd locked the door and she could hardly have unlocked it without my seeing her do it. I'd never taken my eyes off her . . . except when I'd put on records.

My thoughts were still somewhat addled, so I got to my feet and lurched into the bathroom, bathed my head and face with cold water, then thought some more about this mess, the whole thing from the beginning. Until now a lot of things had been twisted around like a loose girdle, but after a couple of minutes all was clear; I'd had my leg pulled all right, I'd been set up, I'd been had.

I went into the bedroom. According to my watch and my best memory, I couldn't have been unconscious very long, but then I've got a thick skull. A very thick skull. My gun and holster were still alongside the record player. I strapped the harness on and went back into the front room for my coat. It wasn't on the hassock; it was gone.

They'd have been in a hurry, at least Garr would have been and it would seem that Lorry Weston was still racing about in my coat. I got another coat from the closet, took a box of .38 cartridges from the dresser and dropped a few extra shells into my pocket, then put a sixth slug in the empty chamber I usually keep under the revolver's hammer.

On my way out I checked the front door. It was my
guess that Garr had used a knife-edge Stillson wrench on
the lock to screw it out. Anyway, it was on the floor. And
so would he be if I found him.

11.
I REACHED the rear of Blake's house without
any trouble, so at least he didn't have radar.
My Cadillac was parked a hundred yards down
the dirt road, unlocked, keys in the ignition and the side
door standing open to save time if I were in a hurry later.
Light slanted from under the partly drawn shade of a
window near me and I could hear the faint sound of
voices. The room, if I remembered the house's layout, was
Blake's bedroom, where I'd talked to him earlier.

In another second I was standing before the window,
peering through it, careful not to touch even the pane of
glass. I'd brought a ring of skeleton keys along, plus a
small metal block and a razor-sharp spring leaf for a
jimmy, but not for windows because it was a foregone conclusion that all of them, and the doors, were wired. I could
see inside easily enough, though. I could see Blake, still
in his robe, Ed Garr—and Lorry. This was the safest place
for them, here in Blake's wired house with several of his
hoods around in case of trouble. It was not, of course, the
safest place for me.

As I watched, Blake stepped in front of Lorry and said
something to her. She stood straight before him, Garr off
to one side looking at her—yeah, she was still in my coat
—and practically drooling. Or maybe in fact drooling.
Then Blake slapped Lorry hard twice, whipping his hand
forward and then hitting her again with a backhand.

A tough man, that Blake. Tough with women. Lorry's
head jerked from one side to the other and she staggered
slightly but straightened while she threw words back at him.

I walked away from the window, revolver ready in my
hand, hammer cocked; but the last thing I wanted to do
was use the gun. One shot and up to half a dozen men,
men with guns, would start charging around shooting their
guns. At me.

The window was closed but its shade wasn't even drawn
and I could see the whole room clearly. This was the room
where I'd seen Martita bound and gagged on the bed. Poor,
helpless Martita. She was still there, but naturally not

bound and gagged. Martita was painting her toenails with red gook, legs twisted awkwardly and her delightfully sensual face screwed up in concentration on the job. No bruise on her cheek, either. By now she'd have washed her face, washed off whatever they'd put on her cheek so it would appear bruised.

The cheek, I remembered now, that she'd pressed against the pillow when I'd come close to her. She'd kissed the noble Galahad's hand, of course—"Shell, thank you (sucker) . . ."—but she'd been damned careful to keep her bruise hidden in the pillow.

So Martita was not an old ex-flame of Blake's, but the new one, the new one who'd come in when he'd kicked Lorry out. There must have been a little leak about what Hershey and I were doing, but the big leak had come after that reached Blake, had been one he'd set up himself: Martita Delgado. The rest was easy to figure. He'd fixed her up with a fake story, complete with authentic-sounding names and dates he could supply, then planted her in the Parker Hotel and made sure I heard about her.

But the big thing was the timing, the bits Lorry had told me about. Martita had been "picked up" by the two men and had checked out of the Parker at seven P.M. last night. But, according to Lorry, Garr and Robb had lifted Hershey's safe about an hour before Robb had come to see her, which would have made it close to nine P.M. And inside Hershey's safe were the statements signed by Willie and Nelson—and Martita Delgado. Blake had gotten Willie's name, and Nelson's, from those statements, but he couldn't have found out about little Martita from them. Not two hours *before* the safe was stolen. He'd known about her all along; if she'd left a forwarding address, it would have been Joe Blake's. Some deal Joe had made with me. No strings.

As I walked toward the front of the house my heart began punching the inside of my chest. On the drive here I'd decided there was only one way I might manage to get inside, and it wasn't through a window or down the chimney but through the front door. I knew there was a big ugly man there. And Ugly would look out the door and see me and yell bloody murder. Maybe.

I went out to the grass near Blake's maroon Lincoln, then turned and headed toward the steps, whistling. I stuck the gun back into its holster and kept whistling through rapidly drying lips, walked up the steps and knocked briskly on the door, bum-de-dum-dum—dum-dum, like a teenage boy calling on a teenage girl, then went back into character and pulled my right fist behind my head about a yard. When I heard movement inside I said, "Telegram," and Ugly opened the door and I punched him on the chin, whereupon he fell down for the second time tonight, caught by surprise even though I had telegraphed my punch. And then I was inside with the door shut behind me and the gun in my hand again.

12. HE'D MADE a small thump when he fell, but it didn't draw anybody out to investigate, so I grabbed him by his shoulders and hauled him over to the corner in shadow. In his hip pocket I found the sap I'd seen there earlier, held it in my left hand, revolver in my right. The house was quiet.

I walked to the end of the short hall, cracked the door there and looked through. Light spilled from the bedroom down the hall on my left. A man came through the door, slammed it violently behind him and walked away from me. It was Blake. He went into Martita's room.

He'd come out alone, but Garr was almost surely still in there. The last time Garr had been alone with a woman he'd been with Martita; but that had been just a bound-and-gagged act for my benefit and Martita hadn't been in any danger. This time he was with Lorry.

I stepped into the hall and walked rapidly to the door Blake had come through, dropped the sap into my coat pocket and put my hand on the doorknob, started turning it slowly. I could hear them inside, hear the two voices, Lorry's high and taut, Garr's mumbling.

The door cracked and a strip of light fell on my face. I held the .38's muzzle against the crack as it widened, my eye a foot above the gun, but I knew unless Garr's back was to me there was going to be one hell of a lot of yelling and racing around and shooting in about five seconds. Because if Garr saw me, gun or no gun, that pig brain of his would send him at me—and I'd have to plug him.

I didn't mind the thought of shooting him at all, but I hated the thought of the noise it would make. The crack widened but I couldn't see them, only hear them, and I began figuring that no matter which way Garr was facing, with Lorry in there he'd hardly notice me. And he hadn't noticed the door moving yet. So I stuck my head through and looked into the room.

Garr's back was to me, his thick arms wrapped around Lorry, pinning her arms to her sides. A yard beyond them was the bed. Lorry was gasping, straining away from him, her face twisted, pained, and her eyes closed. For a moment after I stuck my head inside the room she struggled violently, then she opened her eyes and saw me.

It was almost funny the way her expression froze for a long second, then relaxed and grew a twisted, lipstick-smeared smile. She gasped "Oh—" and for a moment I thought she was going to yell my name halfway to the civic center. But she cut it off and pressed her teeth together. Garr grunted, started to turn around.

I jerked my head back, all my muscles suddenly tense. The gun in my hand started quivering I was holding it so tightly. Garr's voice rumbled, "What's with the door?"

I put my left hand against it, ready to slam it open, holding my breath. But then I heard Lorry's voice. "It didn't shut when Joe slammed it. Don't worry about the door. Ed. Ed, look at me. Please, Ed."

There was a short silence, then she said softly, "That's better. That's better, Ed."

I relaxed a little; she was talking to me, not Ed, telling me that he wasn't looking my way now. She had his attention—and that made me start feeling much better about how this little caper might come out. I reached into my coat pocket and took out the sap again, slipped its leather loop around my left wrist. Because if Lorry had Garr's attention, she was the gal who could keep it. How well I knew.

"Ed, honey," she was saying, "if only you wouldn't be so rough. If you wouldn't hurt me . . . it'd be better, Ed, honey."

I no longer had any doubts at all that I could stick my head inside, and almost gayly I looked, then took a step into the room, eased the door nearly closed. Garr still held Lorry's arms, but she was leaning away from him, smiling up into his face. When I stepped inside, her smile got tighter, but she kept on talking softly.

"Let me go, Ed. I can't get away—and I'm not even

going to try. You'd . . . like it better if I didn't fight you, wouldn't you?"

"Yuh!" Garr said.

He released her arms and she stepped slowly back from him, smiling up into his face. I took a step forward, hoping nobody came up behind me and hit me on the head, and hoping further that, if they did, they missed the crack. Lorry sank down onto the edge of the bed, leaned back—and suddenly all of this struck me as something which had happened before.

"Just half a minute, Ed," she said, and it sounded like a woman whispering to a man in her bed. "Think of me, how I feel. Just a little. Talk to me. A woman likes to hear nice things. Just tell me a nice thing or two."

This, of course, was far beyond Ed Garr's capabilities, but no matter, what there was of Garr's mind was occupied, and his back was to me—getting closer to me at that. Even at this rather precarious moment I felt like grinning, and I was so little worried about the outcome here that I switched the gun to my left hand the sap to my right.

I had wondered back there in my apartment, and later, if Lorry had any idea of what she was doing, and doing to me, or if by then she'd been wearing only my coat for so long that she thought it was a complete outfit. But that question was a question no longer: she knew.

If this thing worked it was going to be about the most poetic justice I could think of. Lorry laughed, leaned back even farther and said a couple words to Garr, and all this time I was walking toward him.

I was moving quietly, tiptoeing even, but I could have been a herd of stampeding stallions and Garr would have paid me no heed. Lorry, in her own way, was a genius; she had a technique which swept all thoughts but one from a man's mind, and that one thought had nothing to do with ears. He wouldn't hear me. He didn't.

13. I WAS SMILING when I raised the sap, then I slammed it down on Garr's skull, and just as I had predicted he fell to the floor. Maybe Garr was a match for two ordinary men, but he was no match for me and Lorry. I had no time to drink in the scenery, or even say to Garr, "How do *you* like it?" because Lorry was off the bed and throwing her arms around me.

"You came for me!" she cried.

"You can say that again!" I cried right back at her. "But that's not all. I also came for whatever's in Blake's safe."

It shocked her a little, but I'd wanted it to. If we were going to get out of here alive I couldn't have her throwing herself all over me. She made men forget things, especially other men, of whom there were plenty still conscious in the house.

"Where's that desk you mentioned?" I asked her. "The one with the safe."

She swallowed, looked at Garr's still body. "Down the hall," she said.

"Let's go."

She licked her lips, glanced at the window I'd looked through a few minutes ago. "Can't we . . . I'm scared, Shell."

"So there's two of us. Forget the window; they set off gongs and skyrockets. We've got to leave by the front door. My car's down the road, anyway. So let's hit that safe."

She hesitated, face tense. I said, "Look, baby, it makes more sense than you realize. We're dead, you for sure, if we don't put Blake clear the hell out of circulation. Eight to five the stuff to do it with is in that desk of his. Or do you want to run for the rest of your life?"

She walked to the door. I followed her out, turned left, caught up with her. "This is it," she said. The first key on my ring opened the door; I shut it behind us, turned on the light. Lorry gasped, but I told her, "We can't fool around in the dark, so let's just pretend we live here."

This was Blake's den. The desk's lower left drawer, Lorry told me. I hauled the metal jimmy out from under my coat and said, "Hang on, honey. Let's hope Blake put so many alarms on the house he figured he didn't need a buzzer on this thing. You remember that combination?"

She gasped, put both hands to her cheeks, then smiled weakly. "Yes," she said, sighing.

There weren't any wires in sight, or bumps in the carpet, but I didn't breathe easily until I'd worked on the door for a full minute without anything disastrous happening. While I pried at the metal plate, using the small iron block under my jimmy for leverage, Lorry talked in a steady whisper, as if too tense to keep quiet.

Part of her words were very pleasant things about me, but part were what Blake had done to her, and said to her. Lorry said that last night, Garr, who hung around Lorry whenever he could, had hung around the Ambassador, suspicious after dropping Robb off there. When Robb came down drunker than seven skunks, which is pretty drunk, Garr made him admit he'd seen Lorry. After that, the combination of Garr's big hands and fists, plus Lorry's Martinis, soon got out of Robb the admission that he'd spilled the story of their breaking into Hershey's place. Garr took Robb to Blake, told his tale, and within half an hour Stu Robb was in his ditch. Garr handled that job himself, but a couple other boys, Dee and a guy named Grant, had killed Willie Fein.

Garr's showing up at the Starlight had been the result of Blake's telling him to keep an eye on Lorry, tail her, but his disgusting arrival at my apartment hadn't been. Blake had, after the Starlight episode, told him merely, "Find Lorry Weston," and knowing I'd been at the Starlight when I'd given her my jacket, Garr had come up with one of his own extremely rare ideas, dropped in on me, and dropped me. He'd then brought me here, to Blake, who wanted to know how much Robb had told her, how much she'd spilled to Hershey.

In another minute I'd sprung the lock on the steel plate before the safe swung the plate out. "Do it fast," I said, and stepped aside. I was getting twitchy, and Lorry's face was whiter than paste. Her lips were parted and dry, but she dropped to her knees, twirled the safe's dial, leaned close to it.

A door slammed and I jerked upright. Lorry snatched her hand from the safe. "Go on," I said sharply. She was beathing rapidly through her open mouth, and her hand shook as she put it on the safe's dial again. She pressed her teeth tightly together, turned the knob slowly, then grasped the small chrome handle and looked up.

Looking at me, she pulled the handle. The door swung open. I pushed her out of the way, pawed inside, slid a pile of papers onto the floor. There was a mass of stuff, letters and photos and photostats, typed documents and sealed envelopes. I pawed at them, found two familiar manila envelopes. One I recognized as mine and didn't look inside, but I tore the other open, made sure it contained Hershey's letters, the stuff he'd been worried about. But the statements were gone. I hadn't expected to find them.

There was noise in the hall. I heard a man yelling. "Joe!" The voice was Garr's. That character had a thicker skull than mine. I started grabbing papers and envelopes, stuffing them into my coat and pants, shoved some at Lorry. I stuck the last thick envelope under my belt and swung toward the door as Garr's feet thumped in the hall, but the sound went away from us, toward the room where Blake and Martita were.

Lorry was saying, very softly, "Oh, oh, oh," her hands, for some reason, pressed over her eyes. "Hang on, honey," I said. "Come on, quick." I grabbed her wrist and pulled her toward the door. "If we're lucky we can make it. It'll take them a little time—"

But already feet were thudding in the hall again, coming this way. It sounded like two men, then one of them stopped and in moments a door slammed. The other guy kept coming closer. They were checking the rooms. Somebody yelled again. It sounded like Blake. "Outside. Get outside! Find that punk's car."

"It has to be the window," I said to Lorry. "Get ready to run. And, honey, there's going to be a lot of noise and commotion, so be ready for it." By the time I'd finished I was at the window, but facing the door, gun pointed at it. Lorry was beside me and I could hear her shallow breathing. She'd kicked her shoes off. The pounding footsteps reached the door; it started to move inward. I fired twice through the wood and heard a man cry out. As the door swung open I saw him reel but he didn't fall. Arms wrapped around his stomach, he staggered out of sight.

I didn't see an inside latch on the window and I didn't waste time looking for one but kicked out the glass, raked the barrel of my gun across jagged shards at the window's base while I jerked Lorry close with the other hand. Everything let loose at once.

14. A CLANGING erupted from half a dozen places, from alarms both inside and outside the house—and brilliant light blazed beyond the window, flooding the grounds. Somebody else in the hall was running this way as I took a fast look at the grounds;

they were still empty. I pushed Lorry at the window and she began scrambling through as the footsteps in the hall, practically at the doorway, stopped.

I fired once and chipped wood from a spot halfway down the door frame, then turned and dove through the window, hit the ground hard. Lorry was running with a woman's awkward, knock-kneed leg swing. I snapped one more shot back through the window and ran after her.

She disappeared around the corner of the house, heading for its front, scared, not thinking—but I couldn't blame her. I wasn't doing much thinking myself, but I was doing a lot of running. A heavy gun boomed behind me as I sprinted around the corner, caught sight of Lorry racing toward that long dirt road, staggering now, already winded. She was heading toward the car. I yelled at her, but she didn't pay any attention to me, and kept on. Then, thirty yards beyond the house, she stumbled and fell sprawling.

A split second after she fell a gun cracked. A spray of dirt geysered into the air yards to her left and I heard the slug ricochet, whining, and smack into one of the trees. The shot had come from my right at the front of the house. I kept running as hard as I could, raising the gun. Then I saw him, standing on the grass past the drive, right arm extended toward Lorry's sprawled body.

I didn't even aim the first one, just squeezed the trigger, then jerked the gun toward him and tried to hold it on him, firing as I went past. The next time I pulled the trigger the hammer fell on an empty cartridge, and that one half-aimed shot missed him by plenty, but it scared him. He jerked as the gun at the end of his extended right arm blasted again, then he dropped to the grass and rolled. I'd been close enough to see his face. It was Dee Tolman.

Lorry was getting off the ground when I reached her. I snapped out the revolver's cylinder, digging into my coat pocket for cartridges, ejected the empty cases and started jamming shells into the chambers while I yelled at Lorry. She was only a foot from me, but the way I was yelling she might have been a mile off in the hills.

"Run, baby, but stay away from the car. Blake sent a man there. Don't—"

She was running, but straight down the road. Straight for the car. I flopped to the ground, snapped the gun's cylinder shut and squirmed around to face the house. Dee was sprinting toward the open front door. He was almost at the steps, but I had time to aim. I shot him in the back. His arms flew out straight from his sides like springs, the gun arcing through the air, and he fell, got up and fell again. He crawled to the first step, then stopped with one hand reaching forward. His legs kicked.

A man trotted around the rear of the house at the spot where I'd been half a minute ago. He was more than thirty yards away but both of us were brilliantly outlined in the light. He yanked his gun hand up and fired three times, rapidly, the slugs kicking up dirt yards from me. I snapped two shots at him, another as he jumped back around the corner. The glass of an upstairs window shattered, fell tinkling onto the drive. I fired twice at somebody up there, then scrambled to my knees, turning to run.

That movement kept me from getting my head squashed. I was halfway up and turned around when I saw the man's legs. They were no more than four or five feet away and moving fast toward me; the guy's arms were over his head, something big gripped in his hands. His arms started down as I dived at him, slammed into muscled thighs hard as tree trunks, knocked him sprawling. Something thudded against the ground where I'd been. As he fell backward I kept shoving against him, jammed the gun's barrel into his body and pulled the trigger. The hammer fell with a dull click as a big hand hit my wrist, knocked the gun from my fingers. The thing he'd held, a big jagged boulder, rolled a few feet away and stopped.

He grunted and reached for my throat with one hand and I saw that it was Ed Garr. He was the guy Blake had yelled at, telling him to find my car—and I wondered even as I clubbed his arm away if Lorry had run into him. I rolled, tried to get my feet under me and was on my knees when he lunged at me, hands reaching—and empty. He must have run out of the house without a gun, so we were even. Even except that he had about sixty pounds on me, several friends who would soon be joining him, and I was a hell of a long way from downtown, a hell of a long way from cops.

A lot of big men are fast, but Garr wasn't one of them. He was just brute strength, muscle piled on muscle, and before his reaching hands touched me I dug my toes into the dirt, shoved myself forward, skidding, twisted over and started getting to my feet on the other side of him as he swung around. Papers spilled from me all over the ground, but I wasn't worried now about those papers. Ordinarily Garr's size and strength wouldn't have worried me too much, either, not with the Marine training and judo and brawling I'd had, but I could see three or four points of movement at the house beyond Garr and I didn't have time to play around to try to set Garr up. Whatever happened had to happen fast; whether Garr slowed me down himself, or I took too much time, the outcome would be the same.

15. I CAUGHT a blurred glimpse of a man and woman running toward the maroon Lincoln. That would be Blake and Martita, and I didn't get it, couldn't understand why they'd be taking off. But another guy was coming out the front door and a third man raced this way alongside the house. Garr was looming over me as I straightened up, his big right fist balled and drawn back.

I knew if I tried to turn and run Garr might get a paw on me and it would be over for me, and Lorry, and Hershey—for all of it. So I left myself wide open, didn't even try to block Garr's blow, let him launch that big fist at my face. But I moved in toward him, left hand stretched open, palm up and stiff, swinging my head a little to the right. His fist scraped my chin, thudded into my neck and spun me, but my left hand dug into his gut, fingers driving deep. My neck and the whole side of my jaw were suddenly numb; I couldn't breathe; but I swung back close to Garr, ripping my open right hand up toward his face. His mouth was open and the edge of my palm caught him under the nose and jarred his head back.

His face went blank. His knees buckled and he might have been dead even then, but I didn't take any chances. I crushed the bridge of his nose with the edge of my right hand, then kicked him in the head as he fell. Light slammed into my eyes and I heard the sound of the Lincoln's motor, saw it swerving across the grass, heading toward the road and me; it cut off the closest man, forced him to dig his heels into the driveway. I turned and ran.

Behind me the sound of the motor grew louder—but I thought that over it I heard the thin, high sound of a siren.

That didn't fit; nobody out here would have called cops, not with papers that would ruin Blake scattered all over the road and even flying from me as I ran. There was another sound behind me, an ugly thud and then the skidding of tires. I knew what that one was: Ed Garr. Blake had run into his body, or over it.

I tossed a fast glance over my shoulder to see the car skidding, stopping. But the Lincoln was already past Garr. I jerked my head around—and stopped running. Far down the narrow road were the headlights of another car, a red light pulsing on its top. And the sound was definite now, a siren wailing high and dropping.

Actually seeing the radio car, cops on their way, made me understand, suddenly, how it happened that they were here, why Blake and Martita had started running long before the siren could have been heard.

It was obvious; I should have known that a man with as much pull and power as Blake would have his alarm system channeled straight into police headquarters, just like many other men or business concerns with plenty to protect. Or to hide. What Blake had wanted to hide, however, was now scattered over a hundred yards or so.

Gears ground and grated behind me as Blake tried to gun his car back and forth in the narrow road, turning around. Near the house men were still running—but away from me and off into the countryside. I grinned, happy to chase somebody else for a change, and ran toward the Lincoln. There was nothing to the rest of it.

Blake stalled the motor and was grinding the starter when I slammed into the door on his side of the car, reached in and grabbed his hair in one hand and his neck in the other. He screamed like a woman as I pulled him out through the open window, and he must have thought Gargantua had him and was going to eat him alive.

The frenzy of the last few minutes had finally caught up with me, and the odds had changed so suddenly and happily that I was practically giddy, chuckling joyfully and shaking Blake like a maracca. After Ed Garr, it was almost a shame to slug this one, but Blake was pounding me, or at least slapping at me, so I clobbered him one in the chops, splitting two of my knuckles and ruining his chops, and he had barely hit the ground when the prowl car slid to a stop alongside us.

16. Cops swarmed out of that buggy like bees out of a hive. There were only four of them, but they came at me so fast that it looked like the whole Hollywood Division. Luckily it was the Hollywood Division, because two of the boys knew me and gaped upon me while saying such things as, "Well, Scott, what the so-and-so is this?"

That was right; they'd come out here to protect Blake.

I said, "Gather up these scattered hunks of paper and you won't have to come out here any more. If you want to see Blake you can see him at Quentin. There's a couple dead guys around here, too." Martita was still in the car, quiet as a mouse, looking straight ahead at a tree. "The girl can tell you plenty if she will—and hoods are still running like madmen out there." I pointed.

Blake's lips flapped slightly as he breathed through them. A little puff of dust eddied around his mouth. For the first time I noticed that he'd left in such a hurry, he hadn't even changed clothes, was still wearing his robe. Man, I thought, what a night. What crazy clothes these characters are wearing. A top-bracket hood flying about in white robe and scarf, and a beautiful babe trotting . . .

I started running toward the Cad.

A cop yelled, "Hey!" and another yelled, "Stop!" but I wasn't about to stop. At the Cad I yanked on the door handle, but it was locked. I banged on the car and yelled, "Lorry! Lorry, you all right? You in there?"

Like a Jack-in-the-box, from somewhere down on the floorboards behind the seat, up popped a mass of blonde hair, a forehead, and two bugging eyes, which I knew were green. Almost as quickly they were gone. Relief swept over me. Then, slowly, up came the eyes, not quite so bugging. Recognition grew in them, and Lorry let out some kind of yip and I thought she was coming through the door at me.

A second or two later she'd opened the door and I immediately sprang through it and stopped her frantic chatter, about running from Garr and locking the Cad, by kissing her thoroughly. Well, you know about those kisses. The next thing I knew, a gruff, booming voice filled with authority was saying, "Hey. Hey, none of that."

I stared at the cop, horrified, and said, "You get out of here!"

He was looking at a star. "Clint wants to see you." He walked back up the road. Clint was Lieutenant Clint

Boyles, one of my friends from the Hollywood Division. Yeah, I thought, I guess he *would* want to see me. I told Lorry to say in the Cad, and lock the doors again, then went to see Clint.

He was talking to Martita. Blake sat in the dirt, leaning against the Lincoln's front wheel. Clint said to me, "What's the score with this gal?"

I said to Martita, "Haven't you told him yet, honey? Hell, you haven't got a gag on now." She had the grace to blush and lower her eyes.

"I . . . I'm sorry, Shell. I didn't know what all was going to happen."

"I'll bet. But I guess nobody knew what all was going to happen."

"What are you talking about?" Clint asked me.

"She'll tell you." I looked at Martita. "You are going to tell him, aren't you, baby? It's the only chance you've got. Maybe you knew all the hell you were starting, maybe you didn't, but tell it all or you're out of circulation."

She didn't say anything. Blake struggled to his feet. "Keep your mouth shut." He lisped.

"Martita," I said quietly, "you've got to make up your mind right now. Spill it all, every single bit you know, and maybe you'll get off easy; but stay clammed and you're sure as hell going to Tehachapi. For a long time. Long enough for your face to get wrinkled. Long enough."

Slowly she put a hand to her throat, dark eyes looking straight into mine. Her fingers moved on her throat as she swallowed.

"There's a lot of bitter old women in Tehachapi, honey. They're all bitter old women up there. Even the young ones."

Almost before I finished she was talking, fast and furious. Blake stepped toward her, but a cop grabbed him. Martita kept spitting words out. They were the right words. Another prowl car had arrived, and officers were going after the vanished hoods. The car radios were busy. I found my empty gun. Two officers gathered up all the papers they could find and I found a couple still left in my pockets. From Clint I got the manila envelope with Hershey's stuff in it; he knew me well enough so that when I told him it had nothing to do with the dope on Blake he let me take it. He was interested in the others, anyway.

And with reason. Blake had used a little blackmail to

keep some of his men, including a couple State Legislators, in line, and there were photostats, legal and illegal documents, evidence of perjury, bribing or being bribed, proof of other extra-legal transactions, even some of the usual photos. I wasn't particularly interested in the individual items, just their overall effect. Hershey's opponent was one of the men Blake had the goods on, so as far as the upcoming election was concerned, there was no doubt that Paul Hershey was in. Blake was in, too; in Q, as the boys at Quentin say, for a few years. The way Martita was still spitting words, it did appear that she might not have a very difficult time. I wasn't too sorry.

I told Clint, "So that's it. Blake set up the Merchants' Union meeting to be sure Hershey would be out of the house while they leisurely searched it. Martita can fill it in." I told him I'd be down in the morning to take care of statements and charges, then said, "You know the whole thing now. How about phoning Paul Hershey and giving him the scoop? Tell him I'll bring his envelope back tomorrow."

"Okay, Shell." He frowned slightly. "Why can't you call him?"

"Well, I'll be doing something else."

Somebody guffawed. Clint looked around and said, "What are you laughing at?" The cop said, "Nothing," and looked at a star. I headed for the Cad, and I didn't walk, I ran.

❖❖❖❖❖❖❖❖❖❖❖❖❖❖❖❖❖

Dead
Giveaway

SHE CAME into my office as if she were backing out of it, a thin, frightened-appearing mouse who looked like the picture taken before the Before picture, and she stared all around the office in a most bewildered way before even looking at me.

"You—are you Mr. Scott? It said on the door— I— oh—"

It says on the door, *Sheldon Scott, Investigations,* but I'd never thought that was anything to crack up about. Not even my appearance—six-two, 205 pounds, stand-up white hair and whitish miniature-boomerang eyebrows, plus a slightly bent nose and a thin slice gone from my left ear— could have done this to her. Life could have. Or jaywalking through the Los Angeles traffic on Broadway one floor below. Or trouble. Well, people come to me when they're in trouble.

"Yes, ma'am, I'm Shell Scott."

I got her seated in the leather chair opposite my desk, then sat down again and waited.

She was about twenty-five years old, possibly less, with muddy brown hair and eyes and complexion. Squint lines of worry etched the skin around her eyes, and the corners of her thin-lipped mouth turned down. Her face was almost expressionless, as if she were trying to keep the features rigid and immobile.

She had been carrying a paper sack in her hand. Now she started to put it on my desk, changed her mind, started again and then let out a little sigh as if she wished she could leave the thing hanging there in the air.

Finally she reached into the sack and took out a bottle of milk. She put the bottle on the edge of my desk, and we both stared at it. I don't know what she was thinking, but I was thinking maybe she was in the wrong office. Next door to me is Dr. Elben Forrest, a consulting psychologist. He's pretty balmy himself, and all sorts of weird characters visit him.

But I didn't say anything except, "What did you want to see me about, ma'am?"

"I—I'm Ilona Cabot," she said. "Mrs. Cabot. I'm married." She paused, her head turned slightly sideways, peering at me from the corners of her eyes. Despite her plainness and drabness, she had a rather sweet look about her. Sweet—but naive, unknowing.

After a pause, she went on, "I've been married four days. And my husband has been—missing since late yesterday afternoon. I hope you can find Johnny. Something bad must have happened to him."

"Johnny's your husband?"

"Yes. Somebody must have hurt him. Maybe he's dead."

Her face didn't change expression, but her eyes, which had appeared shiny as glass, seemed to melt a little, two tears spilling from them and running down her cheeks. They reached her chin and for a second hung oddly from the flesh, like trembling beads, before falling to the dark cloth of her dress.

She went on, "Otherwise, he'd be with me. Maybe whoever's responsible for him being away is—is the same one who's trying to kill us."

"Somebody's tried to kill you?"

"Two nights ago, Sunday night, just about dusk, I was walking to the little store near our place—I live on Robard Street—when the car almost hit me."

"What car was that?"

"Just a car. I can't tell one from another. But it came down the street and, well, it seemed like whoever was driving it tried to hit me."

"Did you see who was driving?"

"No. I jumped and the car just barely missed me. I fell and skinned my leg."

She paused and I nodded encouragingly. I certainly didn't want her to show me her leg. She went on. "At the time I thought—well, that it was just an accident."

"But you don't think so now."

"No." She pointed to the bottle on my desk. "I got the milk from the porch this morning and before breakfast gave some to Dookie—my little cat. She died right away."

Without touching the glass, I took the top off the bottle and smelled the milk. I'm not a poison expert, but with cyanide you don't have to be an expert. The odor was faint, but it was the smell of peach pits.

"Cyanide," I said. "I'm pretty sure." It appeared that Mrs. Cabot was in the right office after all.

I found out what I could about her suddenly missing husband. Oddly enough, she didn't know very much. She'd met Johnny Cabot, it developed, on the seventeenth of this month, Saturday, exactly ten days ago.

I said, "You mean that you'd only known each other six days when you were married?"

She nodded. "It was—all of a sudden." Two more shiny tears oozed from her eyes. And still there was no real change of expression on her homely face. It was as if pressure built up inside her head, forcing the tears out like fluid through a pinpoint opening in a mask of flesh.

"I'm awfully worried about him," she said. "He's all—he's all I've got."

And right then I moved over onto Ilona's side, not just because she was about to become a client, or because she seemed to be in trouble. It was Ilona Cabot's voice when she said "all I've got." Not the words themselves so much, but the sound of them, the twisted, aching sound that she seemed to be trying so desperately to control. The way she said that her husband was all she had it sounded literally true.

Until ten days ago, Ilona had been Ilona Green, living cheaply and frugally by herself in a rented house on Robard Street and working in a secretarial pool at the Grandon Insurance Company on Hill Street. Usually, after leaving work, she said, she stopped for dinner at a cafeteria called Hansen's. That Saturday, ten days ago, she'd been eating when Johnny Cabot joined her at her table. They'd started talking, and from this casual meeting had gone on to a movie and arranged to meet the following day. Three days after they'd met he'd proposed to Ilona, they'd got their blood tests and been married on Friday, four days ago.

Her husband had gone out after dinner last night, she said, about seven P.M., and hadn't come back. He had told Ilona he was a salesman for the Webley Dinnerware Company, but was on vacation; she didn't know where the company was located.

"What about this milk? When is it left at your house?"

"The milkman comes by about five every morning and leaves a bottle on our porch. Between five and a quarter after, usually."

"Uh-huh. And when did you get it from the porch this morning?"

"It was about six."

"So if somebody poisoned the milk, it was probably between five and six this morning." She nodded and I went on, "Where was Mr. Cabot when you almost got hit by that car?"

"He'd gone out for a walk. That was Sunday."

"Uh-huh." She didn't seem to find anything unusual in the fact that her husband had been nowhere around at the time of both attempts on her life. So I didn't mention it. Instead, I asked her to describe her husband.

Her eyes brightened and a smile touched her lips. She sort of glowed. She beamed. The man she described sounded like a composite of Greek gods and Roman athletes, so I asked her if she had a picture of him. She had brought one along in her purse.

Johnny Cabot even looked a little like a Roman athlete. In the snapshot, he was wearing swim trunks, leaning back on the sand with his elbows under him, sunlight glinting on almost as much muscle as tan. The features were sharp, and pleasant enough. He appeared to be a very well-built, good-looking guy about thirty. The expression was a bit surly, though. The dark eyes under heavy brows seemed angry, or resentful. Take him back a couple of thousand years and put him in a different outfit, and he might well have been a Roman gladiator lying on his back in the arena, glaring up at some egg about to stab him with a trident. He was plenty good-looking, and that puzzled me; he and Ilona Cabot just didn't make a pair.

Ilona gave me their address and their phone number. And in a couple more minutes I was hired, for a minimum fee, to accomplish two things: first find Ilona Cabot's hubby, if he was still alive, and second learn who was trying to kill the Cabots—or kill Ilona; I had a feeling that the poison had been meant solely for her. I told her she'd better move to another address temporarily, but she refused, saying that her husband might come home or try to get in touch with her there. I told her to be extremely

careful about answering the door, and that I would phone
or come by later in the day. She said that would be fine,
and left.

As the door closed behind her, I picked up my phone
and dialed police headquarters. I was still talking to
Sergeant Prentiss in Missing Persons when the office door
opened and my second caller of the morning came in. I
didn't even look around for a few seconds, just finished
asking Prentiss to let me know if they came up with anything from his bureau of the morgue on John Cabot,
then started to hang up, and looked around, and dropped
the phone.

This one would have made a pair with Johnny Cabot,
gladiator. Or with Caesar. Or, especially, with me. Maybe
it was just that she benefited so much by comparison, and
that she had entered about fifteen seconds after the dull,
drab one had left, but she seemed to have in abundance
everything that Ilona had not.

2. THIS ONE was bright and sparkling, and her
hair was red, fire-engine red, and that was
appropriate because she would always be going
to a fire. She was about five feet, five inches of spontane-
ous arson leaning forward on the desk, both hands far
apart on its top, and that caused the white blouse she
was wearing to fall away from her body far enough to re-
veal truly remarkable proportions.

"I hope you can help me," she said.

"Help you?" She had great big blue eyes and one of
those mouths best described as ripe and red. It was plain
asking for it.

She went on breathlessly—but breathing, as I took pains
to notice, "Oh, I do hope you can help me."

"I do, too. I—"

"It's men. Men like you. And sex, and all that."

"I—sex?"

"Yes. It's difficult to explain. Perhaps it's because I was
so late getting started. I don't know how I could have
been so casual about men before. Now I—I just want to
hug them and *squeeze*—"

"Hug them and *squeeze*—"

"Like you. I could just hug you! Boy, could I *hug* you!
You must be big as a house."

"I'm only six-two. Hardly a house. What the hell—"

"It's nice, but I can't go around like this all the time. Can't you do something to help me, Doctor? Prescribe something?"

"Honey, I know exactly what will . . . Doctor? What do you mean, Doctor?"

"Aren't you Doctor Forrest?"

"Hell, no," I said disgruntledly. "I'm only Shell Scott."

"Who's Shell Scott?"

"Me. I just told you, I'm Shell Scott—oh, the hell with it."

"What have you done with Doctor Forrest?"

I got up and walked across the room to the bookcase against the wall. I looked at the happy, dumb, multicolored guppies cavorting in their small aquarium atop the bookcase. They crowded up at the front of the tank and ogled me, leaping about friskily, expecting me to feed them. But I merely dipped my fingers in the water and put them, cool and wet, on my temples.

When I'd got pretty well calmed down I said, "I haven't done anything to Doctor Forrest. He is right next door, where he belongs. Where you belong. Where, perhaps, I belong."

She laughed, but then got quiet for a moment. "You must mean I'm in the wrong office."

"Now you got it."

She stared at me, then said almost resentfully, "Well, it's a mistake anybody could have made. Especially when I saw that woman leaving here. That proved it."

"Proved what?"

"That this was a psychologist's office. A woman who looked like that would almost have to be coming out of a psychologist's office. What kind of an office is this, anyway?"

"I'm a private detective."

"Gracious. What would a woman like that want with a detective?"

"She wants me to find her husband, among other things."

"Husband!" She looked shocked. "Husband? I—well, who would have thought she'd have a husband?"

"Lady," I said, "this has all been very new and interesting, but it's time to call a halt. I have work to do."

"You must think I'm an awful goof. It's just that I

had an appointment with Doctor Forrest and was so worried about telling him. I had to grab my courage with both hands if you know what I mean."

"I think I do."

"I'm really not a goof. Normally I'm quite normal. But—well, I'm sorry. If I need a detective to investigate something I'll get in touch with you, Mr. Scott. All right?"

I grinned. "That would be all right even if you *don't* need a detective to investigate something, miss. Is it Miss?"

She smiled. She was really an interesting, intriguingly fashioned female when she smiled like that. "Miss Carol Austin," she said. "Plaza Hotel, Room Thirty-seven, Mr. Scott."

"I'll remember. And call me Shell."

"Good-bye." She walked to the door, then looked back at me. "Shell." She went out smiling.

I sat behind my desk, smiling. Then my eyes fell on the bottle of milk. Ah, yes; Ilona. I went back to work.

3. IT WAS afternoon before I came up with any-thing solid. By then I'd had the milk tested —it was loaded with enough potassium cyanide to kill a dozen people—and had located Johnny Cabot's address. At least it had been his address before he'd married Ilona.

At the Hall of Justice I got a copy of the application for marriage license which had been issued ten days before to Johnny Cabot and Ilona Green. He had, automatically, given his parents' true name and address. Mr. and Mrs. Anthony Cabitocchi lived at Pomona, California. When I called them the Cabitocchis knew nothing of their son's marriage, but were able to supply me with the address at which they wrote him. That was Apartment 12 in the Franklin on Sunset Boulevard between L.A. and Hollywood. By five P.M. I was talking to the manager there. After I'd identified myself and explained why I'd like to look over Cabot's room, the manager let me into Apartment 12, and followed me inside.

The room looked as if it had been very recently used. I asked the manager if Cabot were still living in the room. "Far as I know," he said. "Rent's paid up for another month."

In the bureau drawer I found a stack of photographs. There were about twenty of them each different and all of women. Ilona wasn't one of them. In the same drawer were two clippings from newspapers. One of them, yellowed by time, was brief mention of a paternity case that had been tried here in Los Angeles. A man named William Grant, 26, had been accused of fathering the child of one Mary Lassen, 18, but had beaten the case in court. The other clip stated that William J. Grant had died after a long illness and that services for the "well-known local bachelor-millionaire" would be held on the following Thursday.

A paternity case. I wondered why they were never called maternity cases. I also wondered what Johnny Cabot was doing with the two clippings—but then I hit pay dirt. It was a pay voucher, showing that John Cabot had received his salary from the Westlander Theater.

I'd never been to the Westlander, but I knew what and where it was—and I was very soon going to visit it for the first time. The Westlander was a burlesque house, but it was to the burlesque circuit about what Spike Jones is to classical music, or one pair of bloomers is to the Arabian Nights. On occasion newcomers to the game got their start at the Westlander, but usually the game was almost over before an act hit the small theater on Los Angeles Street.

I headed for Los Angeles Street.

The Westlander was showing a twin movie bill—*Dope Hell of the Sadistic Nudists*, and a film about a real negative thinker, *I Even Went Wrong Wrong*. In front of the small theater were stills from the movies, and nearly life-size photos of the burlesque queens currently appearing here. I bought a ticket from the gal in the booth, turned and took a step toward the entrance, then stopped and blinked, and blinked again.

Opposite the box office was the large photo of a large gal, and even though she was a young and shapely creature, especially in contrast to the others pictured here, and even though she was a long lush blonde with equipment which looked like what we might expect on next year's model, that wasn't why I was blinking.

I was blinking at the name printed on the picture's base—Ilona, the Hungarian Hurricane.

Ilona?

Just a few hours earlier I'd been talking to another Ilona, my client, Mrs. Johnny Cabot, who was the only Ilona I'd talked to in months, maybe even years. I looked the picture of this one over carefully, but she was for sure a different Ilona. I went inside.

In a couple minutes I'd located the manager inside his office. He was a pale, cigar-chewing man named Dent. I identified myself and said, "I'm trying to locate Johnny Cabot. He still work for you?"

The manager nodded and said around his long brown cigar, "Yeah. That's funny, y'know? You comin' here."

"How's that?"

"Private detective, I mean. You're the second one been here in the last couple weeks."

"Oh? Who was the last one? What did he want?"

"Guy named—ah, Wells—Welch, that's it, Welch. Wanted to talk to Ilona. She's just started here, new to the business. He talked with her, then left with Johnny."

"Johnny Cabot?" Dent nodded and I asked, "What did he want with Cabot?"

"I dunno. I just saw them leavin' together."

"When was that?"

Dent checked some records in his desk. "Fifteenth, it must've been," he said. "Johnny asked off on Saturday the seventeenth, for ten days, and that detective guy was here a couple days before that. Johnny just got back today."

"Back? You mean he's here now?"

"Where'd you expect he'd be? Sure he's here."

"I— Did Cabot say why he wanted time off?"

"Just that something important had come up."

I was remembering that Cabot and Ilona Green had met on Saturday the seventeenth. "Okay if I talk to Cabot?"

"Sure. Have to wait a few minutes. He's my singer."

Dent showed me to a box seat at the side of the stage, briefed me on what remained of the show, and left. The chorus was currently occupying the stage. It consisted of about twenty girls, or rather females, all leaping about with complete disregard of the pit band, shaking to the left and shaking to the right, and backward and forward; but the kindest thing I could say about them was that they were no great shakes.

When they trooped off into the wings, a tall, thin, bony

babe trotted listlessly into view, smiling as if it were painful, and proceeded to take her clothes off like a woman preparing to go to bed alone on a freezing night, with only one thin blanket in the house. There just wasn't any joy in it. Her performance didn't make me feel good all over, as the saying goes. It didn't make me feel good anyplace.

Finally it was finished. The chorus trooped back on and began tap dancing to one number while the band played another, and a tall dark guy walked onstage carrying a microphone and its stand. A couple yards in from the wings he stopped, placed the mike before him, spread his arms wide and started singing.

So here, at last, was Johnny Cabot. Somehow I hadn't quite believed Cabot would be there, not until this moment. If the story Ilona Cabot had told me was true, Cabot's being here four days after his marriage, singing in a cheap burlesque house instead of home with his bride, just didn't make good sense to me. Not yet, anyway. But it was the gladiator boy all right. Sharp, good-looking features, heavy eyebrows, thick dark hair. He had that surly look still, I noticed, even though he was smiling most of the time.

But I wasn't smiling. The sounds banging in anguish at my eardrums were coming from Johnny Cabot as if they were escaping. He had a high, squeaky voice that sounded like a musical saw being played in a swamp full of mosquitoes, and his stiff gestures might have been Frankenstein's monster blowing kisses at King Kong.

The girls swung to their right, bent their knees and threw their hands into the air, looking up toward the ceiling, as if they had all seen hairy tarantulas dangling from a crosswalk; then they all spun to the opposite side and did it again, while Johnny cried, "Tem . . . *tay* . . . shun!" It wasn't the right song. Nothing would have been the right song, but Johnny made even "Temptation" sound like something midway between rock-and-roll and rack-and-ruin.

At last it was over. Johnny bowed and beamed to a complete absence of applause, then went offstage. The girls trooped out of sight. I got to my feet, ready to go backstage and talk to Cabot, but a voice cut in over the p.a. system, saying that we had reached the climax of the show—Ilona, the Hungarian Hurricane. I watched it all.

The number was *Diane*, played slowly and deliberately, and Ilona was slow and deliberate in her movements, of which there were a great many, and many of them great. She was tall, wearing heels at least four inches high, with a lot of blonde hair and a lot of blonde skin showing, and she seemed to be enjoying herself almost as much as I was.

Let's face it. Men like to watch women take off their clothes. When the day comes when that isn't true any more, then we will have entered the Mental Age· and will get our kicks at brain operations. But that day is not yet, so I gleefully ogled the last twitch of tassel, the final flick of bead, and then, when Ilona, the Hungarian Hurricane, bounced and jiggled out of sight, I got up and headed backstage for my first words with Johnny Cabot.

4. I FOUND HIM in a small room off a hall smelling of powder and perspiration. A stagehand pointed to the room and when I knocked Cabot opened the door and glared out at me. That is, he looked out at me, but the general arrangement of his features made it appear that he was always glaring, or perhaps on the verge of biting somebody.

He was about my height, but slimmer, with thick wavy black hair and light blue eyes. I'm pretty brown myself, but this guy must have made a career of soaking up sun because he made me look anemic by comparison. Those pale blue eyes were startlingly light in his darkly bronzed face.

He was good looking, all right, but to me, anyway, he had the look of those guys who star in pornographic movies. He looked weak, much more physical than mental, not clean-cut, not pleasant. He stood there smiling at me, and while it wasn't a bad smile, I almost wanted to go at it like a mad dentist. Once in a while you meet guys like Cabot. It's as if odorless skunk waves keep coming out from them at you. I wondered how my client had failed to notice it. But maybe he affected women differently.

He had his shirt off, and thick muscles moved on his chest. It seemed incredible that a voice so thin could come out of a chest so thick. "Yeah? What you want?"

"You John Cabot?"

"Yeah. So?"

I flipped open my wallet and flashed the photostat of my license in front of his face. His eyes aimed at it and barely focused on it as I snapped the wallet shut and stuck it back in my coat. Sometimes, if you do that fast enough, people think you're some kind of important official. Like a policeman.

"I'm Scott," I said brusquely. "Mind telling me where you were this morning? Early—say about three to six A.M."

He said slowly, "I had a supper date. You know, real late. From about one till after six."

"Six in the morning?" That seemed like an odd time for a date of any kind. Well, almost any kind.

"Yeah," he said. "Gal didn't get off until after midnight."

"Get off where?"

"Club out on Beverly," Cabot said. "The—Grotto." He paused. "Say, you're not a cop, are you?"

"Nobody said I was. I'm Shell Scott, a private investigator."

He spat out foul words. "Private! Why, you son—"

"Hold it, friend. You can watch your tongue or the ceiling."

He bit off the rest of his words, but said, "What in hell do you want with me? What's the score?"

"I'm checking up on an attempted murder."

He grinned, unpleasantly. "I haven't tried to kill anybody, Scott. If I had tried, I'd have killed him. Who was the victim?"

"The attempt was made on your wife. Matter of fact, she sent me out to find you."

"Ilona? She sent you? How in hell did she know—" He bit it off.

"How'd she know what, Cabot?"

"Beat it."

"Aren't you interested in an attempt on your wife's life? She thought maybe it was an attempt on your life, too, since somebody poisoned the milk and you might have drunk some. I don't see it that way, but—"

"I got no more to say to you."

"What about Welch?" For a stab in the dark it got quite a reaction.

"Huh?" Cabot's face got almost pale. The blood did leave his face for a while, and that tan over pallor made him look sick. Maybe he was sick. "Welch?" he said. "I—I don't know anybody named Welch."

I grinned at him. "No. You always look like this. You know who I mean, Cabitocchi. A detective named Welch."

He stared at me stupidly. His mouth opened and closed. But then he balled up his fists and stepped toward me, anger flushing his features and making him appear normal again.

I thought for a second I was going to get to hit him, but something made him stop. A sort of crafty look appeared in his pale blue eyes. He took a deep breath and let it out, then said levelly, "Out. Out you go, Scott. You're a private dick, and if you bother me any more, I'll—" he grinned nastily—"call a cop."

Then he just stood there and looked at me grinning. He was right, too. A private detective is merely a private citizen, and if I were to let my emotion rule my knuckles, I could very well wind up in the clink. I left.

I had a lot more to puzzle me now than I'd had when I'd come into the Westlander Theater. I'd found Cabot, all right, but the big half of the job was no closer to a solution; I still didn't know who'd tried to kill my client, Ilona.

The thought of one Ilona led logically to thought of the second one. After half a minute and one more question of a stagehand, I was knocking on another dressing-room door. This time it was the dressing room of Ilona, the Hungarian Hurricane. A voice inside said, "Just a minute," with no accent at all except the feminine one. Then the door opened.

The only similarity between this gal's expression and Johnny Cabot's was that she looked as if she were going to bite somebody, too. But gently. With eclat, verve, abandon. "Yes?" she said softly.

"Yes, indeed, I just saw your act—"

"Oh, good. Come in." I went inside and she said, "I'm just learning, you know. Did you like it? My dance?"

"You bet. It was real . . . likable."

"Wonderful!" she cried enthusiastically, and gave a little bump from sheer joy. "Wonderful!"

Ilona was wearing an abbreviated robe which looked a

bit like one of those shortie nightgowns and fell down
her thighs only about halfway. It was blue, and made a
pretty contrast with her white skin.

"I practice all the time," she said. "You know what
they say, practice makes perfect."

"That one was pretty near perfect right there."

"*Thank* you," she squealed.

"Uh, my name is Shell Scott." I finally got to tell her
I was a detective, and asked her about her co-performer,
Cabot. She thought he was real nice. She'd been working
here only a little over two weeks, and Cabot had been here
the first week only.

So there wasn't much she could tell me about Cabot,
but remembering his reaction to detective Welch's name,
I asked the Hungarian Hurricane, "Do you know a man
named Welch?"

"No." She was walking around the room, snapping her
fingers and everything. "Who is he?"

"Another detective. I understood that he talked to
you here a couple weeks ago. About that long back."

"Oh, him. Yes, sure. What about him?"

"Would you mind telling me what he wanted with
you?"

She was standing in front of the full-length mirror,
leaning slightly back from it and practicing; then she
glanced at me and said, "You don't mind if I do this,
do you?"

"No." I grinned. "Go right ahead."

"I just want to get the rough edges off this movement.
I think I've got most of them off now."

"I'd say so."

"What was it you asked me?"

"I don't remember."

"Oh, yes. About that detective. He just asked me if I'd
ever been in the Bunting Orphanage here in Los Angeles,
and I told him no, and he thanked me and left." Suddenly she let out a wild, high-pitched noise.

"What was that?" I said. "You all right?" She hadn't
even stopped what she was doing.

"Oh, that was just my squeal," she said.

"Your what?"

"Squeal. You know, toward the climax of my act, when
I'm all a-frenzy, I squeal. It adds something."

"I see. Yes, it would add something. Bunting Orphanage, huh? What did he want to know that for?"

"I don't know. That was all he asked me, and then he left."

"You ever see him before?"

"No. Nor since."

"Do you know if he was a friend of Johnny Cabot's?"

"I don't know. Johnny asked me what the detective wanted with me, though—right after the detective talked to me."

"He did, huh? What did you tell him?"

"The same thing I just told you."

She described Welch as about five-ten, slim, with a black mustache and black hair, beginning to get gray. She had no idea where Welch lived, but she didn't think he was a Los Angeles detective.

That was about it. She was almost ready to squeal again, anyway, and as a matter of fact so was I, so I thanked her and went out. Not all the way out, though; Johnny Cabot was waiting near Ilona's dressing room for me. He waved a hand at me and I walked over to him.

"Listen, Scott," he said grimly. "Get something through your head. I don't want no more trouble from you."

This guy irritated me like a slap on sunburn, but I kept my voice quiet enough as I said, "If you don't want trouble, you're sure going at it the wrong way, Cabot."

"Yeah? Well, I'm telling you, stay away from my wife, see? And from me, and anybody connected with me. If you snoop around any more, get in my hair any more, I'll bust your skull."

"Quit wiggling your muscles, Cabot. At least you admit you're married."

"So my wife hired you. Well, you're fired."

"I'll wait till I hear it from your wife."

He glared at me. "It's enough if you hear it from me. You're finished; no more job."

"What are you afraid of, friend? You didn't try to knock off your wife, did you?"

He was burning. "If I wanted to kill somebody. I wouldn't use cyanide, I'd use a gun. And a bullet can poke a hole in you just as easy as anybody else, Scott. Remember that."

He spun on his heel and stalked off before I could

reply. It was just as well; I had rapidly been reaching the point where my next reply would have been to sock him in the teeth. I went out of the Westlander Theater, found a phone booth in a drugstore, and dialed the number my client had given me this morning.

There wasn't any answer to my ring. I frowned at the phone for a moment, then went back to my Cadillac and drove toward Robard Street.

From my client's house and on past it for perhaps a quarter of a mile, Robard was a one-way street. I parked at the left curb and walked up to the front door. There was no answer to my ring, and I'd started to turn away when I noticed the front door was ajar. I knocked loudly, then went on in.

It was a small, neat place. There wasn't anything unusual about it except that it was empty, and on the kitchen table were some dirty dishes, one of them containing part of a lamb chop and some broccoli. A half-glass of milk sat beside the dish containing the meat. It appeared as if whoever had been eating had left in a hurry.

I lit a cigarette and looked down at the kitchen table, thinking. It seemed fairly clear that Cabot must have immediately phoned Ilona after I'd talked to him at the burlesque theater—before I'd phoned her. One word from him and his bride would naturally have flown to him as fast as she could—not even waiting to finish her lamb chop and broccoli.

I was becoming more and more worried about Ilona Cabot. Somebody had tried twice to murder that mousy, sweetly miserable little gal, and I was pretty sure whoever it was would keep on trying. The thought struck me that I had no proof she was still alive.

I kept thinking about that angle as I got into the Cad and headed on down Robard. The first street at which I could turn off was Garnet, and I swung right there. I'd barely straightened the car out when it happened.

I heard the sound of the shot, but didn't react for a second or so. The slug splatted through the glass and I saw the hole suddenly appear far over on the windshield's right side, as the heavy sound of the gunshot reached my ears. For a second or two I looked stupidly at the hole near the windshield's edge, at the white lines radiating from it and spreading like thick cobwebs over the glass. And then I hit the brake pedal so hard that I shoved myself back into the upholstery of the seat behind me.

The power brakes caught and grabbed, tires shrieking on the pavement as the car slid and turned slightly toward the curb. I jerked the steering wheel left, then slapped my foot onto the accelerator again. I straightened the Cad out and let it pick up speed for half a block, then pulled in to the curb and stopped.

I had the door open and was starting through it, right hand under my coat and touching the butt of my .38 Colt, when I stopped. There wasn't much point in charging back down the street like an Olympic sprinter. Whoever had taken that shot at me was almost surely a lot farther away now than he'd been when he let the slug fly at me. Or when she had. A bullet out of the night is anonymous.

But I could count the people who might know that I was going to visit this address on one finger, or two at most if I included Ilona herself. Somebody might conceivably have tailed me from downtown and then waited near the turnoff on Garnet; but it didn't seem likely. So I was extremely anxious to see Johnny Cabot once again.

5. I LOOKED around, but after twenty minutes I hadn't learned anything new. People in a couple of houses admitted hearing the gunshot, or "backfire," but that was as close as I got. I did use the phone in one of the houses and called the Westlander Theater. When Mr. Dent came on and I asked for Johnny Cabot, he exploded.

"What'd you do to him? What's happening. All of a sudden my star singer's gone. Right after you talked to him he lit out and I ain't seen him since."

I told him I hadn't done anything to Cabot and got him calmed down. Finally he promised to keep it under his hat that I'd called, if Cabot did arrive. I told Dent I'd be phoning him again, then drove into downtown L.A. and spent some more time trying to locate Johnny Cabot or Ilona, without success. I checked again at the Franklin, where Cabot still had his apartment, but he hadn't turned up there. The twenty bucks I left with the desk clerk, however, assured me of the clerk's prompt cooperation if and when Cabot or Ilona showed up.

Cabot had said he'd spent most of last night, or rather this morning, with a gal who worked at the Grotto. If that was true, he couldn't very well have slipped the cyanide into Ilona's milk. I headed for the Grotto.

It was a long, low, gray building on Beverly Boulevard. Shortly before eight P.M. I turned my car over to the parking attendant and went inside. The first thing that caught my eye was a colorful poster in its glass-covered case alongside the checkroom.

It was a large photograph of a busty mermaid resting on her back at what seemed to represent the bottom of the sea. Diving down through the water above her was a muscular male in a pair of bikini-type trunks. The mermaid was, typically, fish from the waist down, but from the waist up there was nothing fishy about her. Long hair streamed through the water like black seaweed, and the whiteness of her skin glowed phosphorescently in the greenish water. A shaft of light fell from above her and touched the white, prominent breasts.

Painted letters that looked like seaweed at the poster's top announced that the Grotto proudly presented "The Neptune Ballet" in the Underseas Room. At the bottom of the big card, more seaweed letters announced that Dan Thrip was the Sea Satyr, and Ilona Betun was "Neptuna, the Venusian Mermaid."

Ilona?

Ilona.

Well, I thought, I'll be damned.

I looked at the shapely mermaid again. If the poster hadn't been a photograph, I might have thought the artist was an advertising man accustomed to ludicrous and enormous exaggeration, but this was a photograph, and this gal was quite obviously not my Ilona, not my client. It is sometimes possible for a reasonably attractive gal to appear uglier than a dead skunk merely by removing all makeup and failing to put up her hair. Add a drab dress and a frown, and the lovely of the night before often becomes the goon of the morning after.

But taking it off is one thing, and putting it on is another. What this mermaid had, gals cannot put on; they have to grow. And grow, and grow.

Almost reluctantly, I turned away from the poster and looked around. Several people sat at the bar and tables, drinking and talking. Near me a young couple was having dinner, thick steaks sizzling on metal platters. A haze of cigarette smoke hung in the air.

I found the manager in his office. He was about five-ten, thin, white-skinned, with receding brown hair and an empty cigarette holder stuck in the side of his mouth. He was scribbling on a paper before him. "Yeah?"

"My name's Shell Scott. I'm a private detective." I showed him my credentials. "You're the manager?"

"Yeah. Joe Grace. Detective, huh? What you want with me?"

"It's not you personally. I'd like to talk to Ilona Betun."

"Uh-huh. You're the second detective that's been in here wanting to see her. This wouldn't just be a gag to get close to the doll, would it?"

"No. Who was this other detective?"

"Guy named—Welch, I think it was. Like on a bet."

"Do you know what he wanted to see her about?"

Grace shook his head. "Didn't tell me. Went up and talked to her, that's all I know about it." He looked at his watch. "Just about show time now. You want to talk to Ilona, you'll have to wait till after the show." He paused. "Join me at my table in the Underseas Room if you want to. We'll catch the show from there."

I told him okay, and he led me out of his office and into the room I'd noticed earlier. The Underseas Room was dimly lighted, not large, and probably held no more than fifteen tables or so, but every table was occupied. Imitation seaweed hung from the ceiling, and ornamental nets adorned the side walls. The entire wall directly opposite the door was glass, except for about three feet at the wall's base, and as we got closer I could see that the space beyond that glass wall, extending in for six or eight feet, was filled with water. It was like a high, wide, but narrow aquarium, a room of water.

Soft greenish light filled the room-aquarium, fell on seaweed moving slowly as if touched by delicate currents, on the rippled sand that formed the aquarium's floor. Joe Grace's table was almost against the glass wall, over toward its left side. As he sat down I climbed into a chair opposite him and he asked me what I'd like to drink. I

told him bourbon and water, and he sent the waiter off
for our highballs. The drinks arrived almost before I
could get a cigarette lighted, and I had a gulp of the
barely watered bourbon as Grace said, "Ah, here we go."
Right after his words I heard a soft chord from the band
on a small, raised bandstand inside the entrance. A man's
voice was saying that we were about to witness the first
show of the evening. He told us in hushed, intimate tones
that the Sea Satyr and Neptuna would cavort in the Un-
derwater Ballet for our pleasure, and finally finished with,
". . . the Grotto is proud to present the lovely, the luscious, the exciting—Neptuna!"

There was a fanfare from the combo, then sudden
silence. In the silence a figure plunged through the water
of the tank, trailing silvery bubbles in its descent toward
the floor of sand. Music began again, softly, a weird
melody unfamiliar to me, and the figure slowed as it
neared the sand.

From her waist down, Neptuna wore a closely fitted
fish tail, dark green and apparently covered with metallic
scales. From the waist up she was nude, her breasts
brazenly thrust forward, bare and whitely gleaming.

Neptuna, or Ilona, swam through the water with sur-
prising ease and gracefulness, despite the fact that her
legs were held together by the rubber costume. I couldn't
guess how tall she might be, but she was beautifully pro-
portioned. The green rubber costume clung tightly to
flaring hips, and above them was a sharply indented waist
that accentuated both her hips and the heavy breasts. She
arched her body slowly, easily, twisting in the water, curling around a black rock and then through the thick
grasses.

Two or three times she swept her arms back and rose
to the water's surface, then twisted around and swam
down again. After the last trip up and down again, as
she approached the side of the tank where Joe Grace and
I sat, she swam almost touching the glass and I got my
first good look at her face.

I had never seen her before, but I was looking forward to seeing her again. It was a very pretty face, and
what I could see of the body was sensational, and if
the legs were even halfway nice, this was a tomato who
could model for lipstick, brassieres, hose, or harems.

What I'd thought a big gray rock lying on the sand turned out to be a giant artificial clam. It opened up as Neptuna swam near it. As she rolled over on her back and neatly maneuvered her tail fin past the edge of the clam's shell, it closed suddenly on her and held her captive.

It was neatly done, and there were even a couple startled or frightened yips from women in the audience. Neptuna twisted and jerked as if in a panic, throwing her body from one side to the other, and her white breasts shivered, rolled on her chest, quivered in the water as she jerked and turned.

Then there was another silvery stream of bubbles as a guy in flesh-colored bikini trunks—the Sea Satyr—dived through the water. His part of the rescue didn't take long, since Neptuna had been holding her breath for quite a while, but he hammed it up for fair in the time he had. I was forced to admit, though, that he looked strong enough to handle a dozen giant clams, even with a couple sharks and a swordfish thrown in. He knifed the clam, which freed Neptuna, whereupon she zipped to the surface for air, then down alongside the guy again. She swirled around him and rubbed up against him, and the sight of those big white breasts sliding against his sun-darkened chest was a good deal more sensual than the pictures in movie magazines.

Then the lips of the two undersea dancers met in a kiss. The lights in the tank went out and it seemed as if the water suddenly turned to ink.

Grace said, "How'd you like it, Scott? Pretty good, huh?"

"Yeah. I'll come in and pay the cover charge next time. Thanks for the vantage point and the drinks, Grace." I got up. "By the way, how do I get up to your star's dressing room? I hope I don't have to swim—"

He interrupted, chuckling, "No. I'd better show you, though." Grace led me to the rear of the club and up wooden stairs to the second floor. Three or four doors opened off a hallway there, and he took me to the third one, where he knocked.

There was the sound of bare feet padding across the floor inside, then the door opened and Neptuna was looking out at us.

Grace said, "This's Shell Scott, honey. Private detective. Help him out if you can. Don't want anybody raiding the joint."

"Sure, Joe." She glanced at him as he turned and left, then looked back at me. "Come on in." The voice was deep, throaty, soft. Even if she were to shout, I thought, that voice would have warm whispers in it.

She stepped aside and I went into her dressing room. As she closed the door behind us I got a glimpse of a big dressing table with a huge mirror over it, a wall closet with its sliding door partly open, a yellow bamboo screen between the dressing table and closet, and the gleam of light reflected from the surface of water at floor level on my left. But then she'd stepped up beside me and I was looking at Ilona—Neptuna—again.

Up close she looked even better than I'd expected. The big eyes were dark, with black brows above them like smears of midnight on her smooth white forehead. The red lips were full, half parted. She wore a thin white robe and held a white towel on top of her head with both hands. The pose did nothing to ruin the robe's appearance, though it pushed it quite a bit out of shape, emphasizing facets of Neptuna's figure that were already quite emphatic. She wasn't a very tall girl, but she had such an abundance of curves that, even if she'd been six feet tall, they would have been enough to stretch out and cover everything most satisfactorily.

"Mr. Scott, is it?" she said pleasantly.

"Shell. No need to be formal."

"Not in this outfit." She smiled. All this time she was rubbing the towel over her hair, presumably to dry it, and that caused quite a commotion in the robe, and quite a commotion in me. Thick clumps of black hair escaped from the towel and hung down on one white-covered shoulder.

"I caught your act," I said. "First time. It was sensational."

"You liked it then?"

"Yes, indeed." I tried a gentle sally. "Any time you need a new partner—"

"I know. You'll start holding your breath." She didn't say it in a sarcastic way, though, but rather as if it were something she'd heard too many times already. She was bored with me.

"I imagine you get a lot of offers from people who can't swim."

"I do." She deftly tied the towel around her head, then cinched the robe's belt more tightly about her waist. She smiled again. "But I turn most of them down."

"Most, huh? How about Johnny Cabot?"

"Johnny? What about him?"

"You do know him, then."

"Sure. Is that why you came up here to see me?"

"One reason. When was the last time you saw Johnny —you don't mind the questions, do you?"

"Certainly not. I saw Johnny last night."

So here it was. Cabot had been telling the truth, or else this lovely was lying, and I didn't like that thought at all. But something was real crazy here; maybe the guy was goofy for Ilonas.

"That would have been after you got off from work?" I said.

"Yes. My last show's at midnight. He picked me up about twelve-thirty and we had something to eat, and talked, you know. Then he dropped me at my apartment at maybe six."

"When did you meet him?"

"Couple weeks ago, about. We went out the night we met, and the next night. But then I didn't see him until last night."

"That's understandable," I said.

"How do you mean?"

"Well, he got married last Friday, and that kept him busy for two or three nights."

I was watching for the reaction, and it came slowly, but it came. It was, however, normal enough for a gal like Ilona Betun, assuming she wasn't really hot for the guy. She frowned, started to speak, then stopped. Slowly she said, "Married? But he—is this a joke?"

"No. He got married four days ago."

"Well . . . what has he been doing with me—I mean, why did he go out with me?"

"I'm curious about that, myself."

She shook her head. "This is a little too much. I thought . . ." She paused, then went on, "Well, he's been trying to make me believe he's in love with me."

"I wouldn't be surprised if he is."

She looked at me, frowning again. "That doesn't make sense."

"In a strange way, maybe it does. But it's too complicated to go into now. There's one other thing. Did you recently talk to a man named Welch? Another private investigator?"

She nodded. "Sure, I've even got his card around here somewhere. Isn't it funny—you just asked about Johnny, then about Mr. Welch, and I met them both on the same day."

"That is a little funny." I asked her to describe Welch, and it was the same description I'd got from the Hungarian Hurricane. I said, "What did Welch want to see you about?"

"The funniest thing. He asked me if I'd ever been in some kind of orphan's home. Of course I hadn't, and I told him so. He asked my age and where I was born and I told him." She shrugged. "And he left. What's it all about?"

"I'm not sure. But I'm getting an idea. This orphanage, could it have been the Banting?" I purposely mispronounced it.

"Yes . . ." She nodded slowly. "That's about—Bunting. That's what it was, Bunting."

"You remember what day it was that Welch came here? And that you met Cabot?"

She thought a minute. "It was either the fifteenth, or not more than a day off either way."

"That's good enough. Johnny knew this Welch, then, huh?"

She looked a little puzzled. "Not that I know of."

"Then you didn't meet them at the same time?"

"No. The detective came here before my first show. And I met Johnny after the last show."

"Welch ever explain why he asked you about the orphanage?"

She shook her head. "He was up here only a couple of minutes. I had to shoo him out so I could get ready for my act. He did say that I was the wrong Ilona, then he thanked me and left."

So both the Hungarian Hurricane, and Neptuna, had turned out to be the wrong girl, the wrong Ilona. That pretty well told me who the right Ilona was.

6. Now that our interview was about over, I looked around again. Two or three inches below floor level, at the left side of the room, water moved gently. It seemed quite strange to see a room with part of the floor wet and liquid, which was the impression I got. I said to Ilona, "So that's the stage for the floorshow. It looks a good deal different from down below."

"I'll bet it does. You know, I've done that act hundreds of times, but I don't know what it looks like."

"Logical enough. Take my word for it, though—you look gorgeous. The whole act is terrific."

"Such enthusiasm!" She smiled. Then she said, "It's almost two hours until the next show, and I don't usually sit around in *nothing* but a robe." I felt sure that she had purposely emphasized the word "nothing." "So do you mind," she went on, "if I get into something more comfortable?"

"No." I was grinning. "Of course not."

Her own smile was pretty close to a grin as she turned and walked away from me. My hopes were pretty high, but then I remembered the bamboo screen. I remembered because Ilona went behind it, then turned to face me. The top of the screen came just an inch or two below the tops of her shoulders. And now I noted, too, that the strips of bamboo were not right up against each other. That is, there were small spaces between them. I could see little strips of white that were her robe. Then, with one easy movement she pulled the robe from her shoulders and let it fall to the floor behind her.

Before, I had seen little strips of white that were Ilona's robe. Now I could see little strips of white that were Ilona's.

It wasn't an awful lot, but it *moved*. Ilona stepped a short distance to one side and reached for something, then bent down and stepped into it. She reached again and slipped a blouse over her head, then reached once more and stepped into what was obviously a skirt. I counted very carefully, however, and she reached only three times.

Then she stepped out from behind the screen and walked barefoot a few feet from the screen, and even if I had not counted, I would still have known she'd reached only three times. Suddenly Ilona stopped, put her hands on her hips, and looked at me. "Well," she said, "you look like a man who plans to come back for the second show."

That snapped me out of it." "No, ma'am, I have work to do."

She chuckled. "Don't be stuffy. I was hoping you did plan to be here. I thought I might put in one little fin flip just for you."

"It might be your fin, Ilona, but it would be my flip." She smiled. "That's better."

"Seriously, I do have a lot to do in the next few hours, but—well, a man can't work all the time. Perhaps we could—" I stopped as a thought struck me. "Johnny Cabot isn't planning to pick you up tonight, is he?"

"I should say not! After what you told me? Nothing was said about it last night, anyway. Besides," she added frankly, in music to my ears, "I'd much rather be with you." She paused, then went on slowly, "I'll be around a while after two. Just in case you get all your work done." She smiled widely. "Sometimes, you know, I wait till the club is closed and locked, and nobody but me is here, and I have a little swim all by myself. Practice the new act."

"Swim . . . by yourself . . . here?"

She nodded.

"Well, that's—interesting." I changed the subject. "I'd like to talk with this Welch. You know where he lives? Or where his office is?"

"No."

"He a local man?"

"I don't know that for sure, either. But I think he was from out of town. We just had a real short talk, and he didn't tell me much except his name—I remember he said his first name was Harry. Harry Welch."

I thanked her and went out. Downstairs again I hunted up Joe Grace and asked him, "When Welch—the other detective—came in and talked to you, was he alone."

"Let's see. Was when he talked to me. But I think he came in with a younger guy. Yeah, they watched the show and had dinner."

"Do you remember what this other guy looked like?" He shook his head, and I showed him the picture I carried of Johnny Cabot.

"Sure," Grace nodded. "I remember now thinking he was even more tanned than Dan Thrip. And them pale blue eyes—yeah, that's the one it was. What about him?"

"I was just curious. I'm real anxious to see him. Thanks again. I'll send in some customers."

He grinned at me as I left. Well, Cabot had hit the Grotto, then, in the company of Detective Welch. The longer this day lasted, the more puzzled I got. But a ray of light was beginning to filter into my thoughts now. There wasn't anything especially strange about there being three—or even three hundred—gals named Ilona in Los Angeles. But it seemed odd indeed that Johnny Cabot should know all three of them. More—he worked with one, dated another, and was married to the third. My running into one Ilona after another had sort of staggered me for a while, because I'm extremely leery of coincidence. But when I ignored coincidence, the light began to filter.

The reason that Cabot knew three gals named Ilona, obviously, was because he'd made it his business to meet them and get to know them. Two of them, anyway. He'd been working with the Hungarian Hurricane for a while, and that would explain his knowing her. But the other two he had managed to run into on purpose. On the 15th of this month he had met Ilona Betun. On the 17th he had met Ilona Green—whom I now thought of as the "right" Ilona—and on the 23rd he'd married her.

There was food for thought in those items, and mainly it made me anxious to find Cabot and his bride—and Harry Welch. I put in a call to the house on Robard Street, but there was still no answer there. Dent was still fuming at the Westlander. A call to the desk clerk at the Franklin got me the information that Cabot hadn't been in.

Harry Welch wasn't in the L.A. phone book or City Directory. I called half a dozen detective agency heads whom I knew personally, and several other investigators I knew by reputation, but none of them had ever heard of Harry Welch. The Bunting Orphanage, at least, was easy to find. The phone book listed it as at 7230 Orange Drive.

It was only eight-thirty P.M., so I phoned the place and talked to a Mr. Simpson. Judging by his voice, Mr. Simpson was about a hundred and eighty years old, and ready to give up the ghost. It was a voice always on the verge of saying good-by. But Mr. Simpson said, sure, he'd given a detective named Welch some information and yes, it would be all right for me to come out and talk to him.

I parked at the curb and walked up a cement path to steps before the wooden porch. The stairs creaked like rheumatic bones, sighed softly as I walked up on to the porch. At the right of the big door, above the push button of the bell, a small weathered brass sign said, "Bunting Orphanage Home."

Mr. Simpson answered my ring. He was little over five feet tall, with accents of white hair on his pink scalp, and a narrow face, but with brown eyes that were still alert and merry. I told him that I was Shell Scott, the man who had just phoned him, and explained why I was here. Yes, he remembered about the other detective. After a few questions, to get him started, he told me all he knew about Welch and the detective's purpose in visiting the orphanage. It fitted well enough into the pattern that had so far developed.

Welch had told him, Mr. Simpson said, that on April 7th twenty-two years ago, a seven-month-old girl had been turned over to the Bunting Orphanage. The detective wanted to know what had happened to the girl and where he could find her now. Mr. Simpson went on, in his quavering, soft voice, "Well, I checked the records and found the one he was after. Baby was brought here by the mother, Mary Lassen. She killed herself."

"Mary Lassen committed suicide? When was that?"

"About a week after she left the infant here. Baby was born out of wedlock, and the way I figure it, the daddy didn't want nothing to do with either of them. Not then. Must of been somewhat of a strain for the woman. But the funny thing is, the father's the man that set the detective to looking up the girl."

"Who's the father?"

"Well, he's a man named William Grant—that is, he *was*. He's been dead and buried for some weeks." Mr. Simpson went on to say that it was because of Grant's death—he thought, but wasn't sure—that Welch had come looking for the girl. Unfortunately, Simpson said, he hadn't been able to give Welch much help, because some of the orphanage records had been destroyed about ten years ago, and among them were the records of the girl's adoption. Thus Mr. Simpson had been unable to discover the name of the people who had adopted her.

"How about Welch?" I asked. "Did he tell you where he was from? Or where he was staying in town?"

Mr. Simpson shook his head. "Didn't tell me anything."

"Do you remember when he was here?"

"I checked after you called and asked about him. It was the twelfth. That was a Monday, little over two weeks back."

I had just one more question. I knew the answer, of course, but I asked it anyway, for corroboration. "You still haven't told me the girl's name."

"She didn't really have a last name till somebody adopted her. But her first name was Ilona."

7. I GOT BACK to my apartment a little after eleven P.M., having tried again, without success, to locate Johnny Cabot or his wife. I parked across North Rossmore from the Spartan Apartment Hotel, crossed the street, went inside, and trotted up the steps to the second floor. And as I reached the top I heard what sounded like somebody else trotting behind me.

I turned around in time to watch Carol Austin bounce up the last few steps. She stopped and looked up at me, panting a little. "Gracious, you move fast," she said.

"Well, hello. What are you doing—"

"You said I could see you. At your office, remember?"

"Yes, but I hardly expected you to show up here. How did you know I lived . . ." I let it trail off, remembering that this gal might conceivably do almost anything. She still looked as if she were going to a fire; even better, I decided, than she had this morning.

Carol Austin seemed to have dressed with more care, applied her makeup even more expertly, and of course she still had all the items which I had so happily itemized this morning; consequently she was a very tasty-looking dish indeed. So even though I was mentally shaking my head at her, I was lost.

There was a kind of hurt, bewildered look in her wide blue eyes, and she said slowly, "Is something the matter, Mr. Scott? Shouldn't I have come here? I looked you up in the book and got your address, and waited down in the lobby, and you'd said it was all right to come see you even if it wasn't for a case, and I . . ."

"Oh, that's all right," I said with enthusiasm. "Anything—everything's all right. Why, I'm happy you could make it."

"Oh, good!"

"Well, there's no point in just standing here, is there? My apartment's right down the hall, so why don't we—"

"Oh, that *would* be fun," she said.

The next twenty minutes were, while a bit disjointed, delightful nonetheless. Carol—after a couple of minutes it was Carol—seemed to think mine was a fascinating life, and wanted to know all about my work.

I explained to her that it was well she hadn't come here to hire me, because the case on which I was now engaged was occupying most of my time.

"What case? I didn't know— Oh, you mean that woman who was leaving your office this morning? You said her name was Ilona Cabot or something, didn't you?"

"Yeah, that's it." We were both sitting on the chocolate-brown divan in my front room. But we were at opposite ends of the divan, so we were yards apart. The divan is big enough to sleep on, or anything.

"Gracious," Carol went on. "Weren't you looking for her husband or something? Did you find him?"

"Yeah, and lost him. But let's not talk shop, Carol."

"Would you think I was awful if I asked if you had anything to drink here?"

I sprang to my feet. "What would you like? Bourbon? Scotch? A Martini, Manhattan—"

"Oh, my, I just meant a Coke or something."

"Nonsense. Though I have Coke."

"Well, all right. A Coke."

"But—"

"With just the teensiest bit of Scotch in it."

"Fine. A Scotch-and-Coke coming right up . . ."

That was such a goofy-sounding drink, like bourbon and beet juice, that it suddenly reminded me of how she'd happened to wind up in my office this morning. I said, "Ah, Carol. How did you make out with Doctor Forrest?"

"Oh, fine. He gave me a pill. You know, to sort of—sort of calm me down."

"And did it calm you down?"

"Uh-huh. I'm fine now. Show me where everything is, and let me mix the drinks. All right? That would be fun."

She got up, took me by the hand and accompanied me to the kitchenette. I watched Carol mix her sticky concoction, then supervised her preparation of a sensible bourbon and water for me. Sensible, that is, except that she managed to slop even more bourbon than I'm accustomed to into my drink.

We got settled again, and I had a glug of my drink and relaxed. There wasn't a great deal of conversation as we finished our drinks, then Carol went alone into the kitchenette to mix a couple more. It seemed to take her quite a while, but I had that much more time to concentrate on problems this case had presented.

When Carol joined me again, I had a small sip of the new highball, then sat it on the coffee table. I was still cudgeling my brain from time to time in the hope of figuring out how I could locate detective Harry Welch. And suddenly I knew.

I'd known all along, if only my memory had functioned. But the salient information had come to me when my mind had not exactly been screwed to the sticking point. I remembered now that while I'd been upstairs in the Grotto, talking to the shapely Neptuna, she'd mentioned that Welch had given her one of his cards. Later she'd said that she had no idea where Welch was staying. But there wouldn't have been any reason for him to leave the card unless his address had been on it. "It's still around here someplace," she said, I remembered now.

I grabbed the phone, looked up the Grotto in the book and dialed. Carol said, "What bit you?"

Joe Grace answered at the Grotto. He told me Ilona was about to dive into her act, but I explained what I wanted and Grace said he'd check with her, if there was time, before the show.

"Thanks, Grace," I said. "I'll be down in a few minutes."

As I put the phone back in its cradle and got to my feet, Carol picked up my drink and walked closer to me. Then she handed me the dark highball and said, "Here. Relax and have your old bourbon."

"Haven't got time. I'm leaving."

"Oh, Shell. You can't ply me with liquor like this and then leave."

"I didn't ply you, you asked for it. Besides, I can feel

that first one too much already, and I've got work to
do."

"The work can wait, can't it? Please, Shell. I'm enjoying myself."

"Sorry. I'm enjoying myself, too, but—"

"I haven't enjoyed myself so much in a long time. And
my pill's wearing off." She stepped close to me, put her
arms on my shoulders and looked up at me. I had for a
second there thought she probably couldn't get any closer,
but I was wrong. She got quite a bit closer. "My pill's
wearing off," she said in a low, husky voice. "I can tell."

"I can tell, too. And don't forget, I haven't had any
pill."

She was sort of squirming around, and her hands went
up behind my neck and traced little paths of cold in my
suddenly heated skin, paths like small fire-breaks in the
midst of conflagration, and I came very close to weaken-
ing.

She said, "I'm so glad I met you, Shell. I don't want to
let you go now."

"I'm practically gone. I mean, here I go—I'm—good-
by."

The phone rang. I jumped for it and got away from
Carol. It was Joe Grace again. "Scott," he said, "I just
remembered you mentioning that guy who came in with
Welch. The guy with the tan, and the pale blue eyes. I
just saw him come in."

"He's there now? Anybody with him?"

"He came in alone. Didn't say boo to me. Went upstairs. Probably to see Ilona, but I figured I'd call you
right off, seeing how you said you were anxious—"

There was undoubtedly more, but I didn't hear it. I
dropped the phone onto its hook and headed for the
door. Carol yelled, "But what'll I *do?* My pill *is* wearing
off."

"Take another one," and out the door I went.

8.

I LEFT my car in the Grotto's lot, and raced to
the club's entrance and inside. The Underseas Room band was playing the weird number
which introduced the show. I ran up the back stairs three
at a time and as I got to their top and ran down the
hallway toward Neptuna's dressing room I saw husky Dan

Thrip, in trunks, standing outside her door, apparently waiting for the musical clue that would be his signal to go in and dive into the tank. Cabot wasn't in sight anywhere.

I sprang past Thrip, opening the door and going through as he yelped, "Hey, what duh—" but then I saw Neptuna. Or rather her tail. She had just dived into the pool and was entering the water.

And then I saw Cabot.

He must have been talking to Ilona until the moment she dived, because he was just turning toward me. Those pale blue eyes got about twice as wide as normal in his dark face when he lamped me but then they narrowed again as I jumped toward him. He balled up his fists, stepped toward me, and launched his right hand at me like a brown rock. He didn't have any intention of starting a conversation, he simply wanted to bust my skull.

But I had not been charmed by Cabot, either, so I felt almost gleeful as I pulled my head slightly aside as I got close to him and that brown-rock fist, bent forward a little, and slammed the knuckles of my left hand into his stomach. Or rather, onto his stomach. It felt like I'd busted my hand. That stomach of his was like a piece of corrugated cast iron.

Cabot didn't even grunt, but his fist whispered past my ear without doing any damage. He staggered back a step, then moved around me, lips pressed together. He feinted twice with his left, then slammed his right hand at me— and he was wide open.

I bent my legs and leaned a bit to the side to let that looping right whistle past my face, then straightened up and pivoted, slammed my right fist against the side of his chin. It made a fine, a dandy noise, and he staggered backward, his arms flying up loosely in front of him. I had him, and knew that just one more punch would settle this altercation if it wasn't already settled. And when Cabot came to, then I'd ask him all the questions about Welch, and his wife, and the other Ilonas, and the shot at me, among others.

But that hard-thrown right hand pulled me around a bit, left me a little off balance, and I moved my left foot back about six inches to steady myself. That was the wrong thing to do. My foot was resting on *nothing*.

The horrible realization swept over me even as I flailed
my arms trying to regain my balance. But it was too late.
Almost involuntarily I gave a short hopping movement,
and then I was flying backward into wetness. Wetness,
and a sickening realization. My eyes were closed, but even
without looking around I knew where I was. I knew what
I was, too, and it was almost unthinkable, certainly un-
printable.

When I opened my eyes I could see quite well, even see
the glass wall of the aquarium in which I was hanging,
sort of stunned and unbelieving. I couldn't see outside, but
I could imagine with dull horror the expressions fixing
themselves on customers' faces out there.

Below me was Neptuna, the mermaid. She was swooping
through the water and curling around a rock quite gracefully, entirely unaware of what dangled here above her
head in wet tan slacks and a sopping brown sports coat.
Undoubtedly she had not the slightest suspicion that anybody—especially me—had yet followed her into the water,
and she was looking happy, almost smiling, as she arched
her back down there and started to glide up through the
water.

But she spun slowly around and lamped me and her
arms flew up over her head like springs, her mouth opened
wide, and her legs split through the thin rubber mermaid
skin as if it were Kleenex. She froze in a strained, awkward position, floating there in the water with her arms
and legs akimbo, bent into the approximate shape of a
swastika, and looking very much like an arthritic Balinese
dancer engaged in drowning.

Then she screamed. Bubbles ripped out of her mouth
like horrified silver balloons and popped up past her head.
In that moment Ilona seemed to gather enormous strength
from somewhere, and all of a sudden her arms and legs
were moving as if she had six of each. As she shot past
me, I came to my senses and took out after her. My head
popped up past the surface of the pool just as Ilona was
clambering out, inches from me. Only inches. It was a sight
that, unfortunately, I couldn't appreciate to the full right
at that moment, but it was often going to flash back into
my memory and jangle all my nervous nerves like pink
lightning.

Then she was on her feet and racing away.

"Ilona!" I shouted. "Wait, it's me, Shell Scott. It's me!"

For a second I didn't think my words were likely to have any effect on her, as if the sight of me had drained her of further power to react in any way except running, but then she stopped suddenly and sort of jerked. She quivered slightly like a woman who had stuck her finger into an electrical outlet, and slowly turned. She stabbed me with a strange, anguished gaze as I rose dripping from the water.

"Ilona," I said. "I'm—I—what can I say?"

She stared at me.

"Well," I said a bit pettishly, since I was pretty uncomfortable to begin with, "I didn't do it on purpose, you know."

There was some more silence, and finally I asked, "Did you find the card?"

"Card?" At last she spoke. Her voice was dull. "Yes, I found the card. I didn't know you wanted it so badly," She was still staring at me.

Dan Thrip was staring at me, too. He stood outside in the hall, eyeballing me through the open doorway. His chin was hanging down two or three inches, which was about as far down as it could hang, and his long arms dangled at his sides. He was looking from one of us to the other, with a fixed stupidity of expression, and not a glimmer of understanding in his blank eyes.

His cue had come and gone long ago. He had heard those musical notes that said to him, *Go Into Your Act, Dan,* but somebody had changed the act. Everything was all fouled up. He was bewildered, nonplussed, unsure of himself.

The events of the last minute or so had, understandably, occupied my mind to the exclusion of everything else. Consequently I had forgotten all about Johnny Cabot. But suddenly I remembered that he should be lying without a wiggle on the floor. He wasn't even in sight.

"Dan," I said. "What happened to the guy who was in here?"

It took him a while to answer, but at last in a few, halting phrases, he indicated that a guy had come racing out past him and downstairs, very obviously in a big hurry —which told me that by now Cabot would be about a mile from here. I started to race out after him anyway, but then stopped, knowing that chasing the man now was useless.

I said to Ilona, "What did Cabot want with you? What was he doing here?"

She had practically recovered her senses and poise by now, and she said, "It was about you, Shell. He just came in without knocking or anything and asked if you'd been in to see me. When I told him yes, he seemed real angry, started swearing and all."

Apparently Cabot had remembered telling me he'd been with a girl from the Grotto this morning, and hadn't liked the idea of my coming here. "He say anything else?"

"Yes, he told me if I saw you or heard from you again to deny that I'd been with him or ever met him. He seemed pretty worried about it."

"He would be."

"I'll get that card," Ilona said. "Don't—do anything." Then she looked past me and seemed to notice Dan Thrip for the first time. She slammed the door in his face. It slammed not more than two inches from his nose, but as far as I could tell he didn't move at all.

The recent events had probably put him nearly into a state of shock, but it finally dawned on me that the real push into trauma must have been his first sight of Ilona, the mermaid, without her fishtail, most of which was somewhere in the pool down below. Only wispy segments of it still remained.

Ilona and I both stood there looking at each other and dripping, and then she chuckled. The chuckle turned into a laugh, and after a moment I joined her. When we caught our breath again, we were both back to normal.

I was so back to normal that I had got quite close to her indeed, and she reached up and put both hands on my shoulders. It was about the same movement that Carol had earlier made, but this time it filled me with all sorts of desires, and not one of them was the desire to leave.

It seemed the most natural thing in the world for my arms to go around her, and her fingers to tighten on my shoulders, and her parted lips to get closer to mine, and then meet them eagerly, almost harshly. It was delightful. It was also, there is no doubt, one of the sloppiest kisses in my kissing history.

We mashed together, dripping, squishing, and gurgling.

Since she had almost nothing on, I was doing most of the dripping and squishing. But she was gurgling. There was really quite a bit of sound there for a minute or so, like those hi-fi records of heartbeats and joints popping. I even heard a far-off pounding.

Then I realized the pounding wasn't so far off. Somebody was running down the hall. Then I heard Dan Thrip saying, "No! You can't go in. She hasn't got no clothes on."

Ilona leaned back an inch or two and looked up at me. "Why, that's true," she breathed in mock surprise. "How could I have forgotten?" Then she stepped back and said, smiling, "Now, don't peek," and walked slowly, beautifully, artistically, to the bamboo screen and behind it. I felt a bit weak.

In a few seconds she came into view once more, wearing that white robe again, and at almost the same instant the door burst open. Joe Grace leaped into the room, his face livid. He pointed a finger at me. "You!" he shouted hoarsely.

9. DAN THRIP came in and grabbed Grace, who told him he was fired, but then Thrip noted that Ilona was clad in her robe and he calmed down, and Ilona cooed a few words at Joe Grace and said everything would be all right. Her robe fell slightly open as she leaned toward him, but she quickly grabbed it and pulled it together; after that, however, when Ilona asked them to please leave, for just a little moment, they both went out meekly. During all that I managed to elicit the info from Grace that Cabot had gone tearing through the club and outside minutes ago.

As the door closed, Ilona reached into the pocket of her robe and pulled out a small white card. "I found this just before you showed up—Joe said you'd be by. Is this what you wanted?"

"Uh-huh." The name Harold Welch was printed on the card, with the word "Investigator" below the name. That was all, but written across its back was "Rancho Cottages, Cottage 12."

Ilona said, "Shell, maybe if you get all your investigating done real fast, you might get back here before closing."

"A brilliant thought, but highly unlikely."

"Well, you try, anyway. But right now you'd better go—Dan and I still have a show to do."

I shuddered. I looked down at my dripping clothes and shuddered again. A sudden pain rippled through my stomach and I bent slightly forward, wincing. Dizziness swept over me momentarily.

Ilona said, "What's the matter, Shell?"

"I don't know. Must have bent some muscles . . ."

"You should be sprained all over."

"Maybe Cabot clobbered me when I wasn't looking. No, I understand—I swallowed some water and there wasn't any bourbon in it. The shock shattered my nervous system."

She was smiling, but I wasn't. I had barely noticed similar sensations a couple times in the last few minutes, but in the movement and excitement I'd paid no attention. I did feel a bit dizzy, but that wasn't too unusual. I told Ilona good-by and to put on a sensational act, and left.

Half an hour later, after looking up the Rancho Cottages in the phone book, I'd found the place and was talking to the sleepy owner. At first he'd ogled my wet clothes, but I told him I'd fallen into the lake at Mac-Arthur Park and that seemed to satisfy him. The Rancho was a twelve-unit motel-type spot off Grange Street about five miles from downtown L.A. The owner, a man named Brand, said he remembered Mr. Welch, but he hadn't seen him for over a week; Welch had left word that he wasn't to be disturbed, even for maid service, unless he asked for it.

Mr. Brand went on, "I think he had a babe livin' with him."

"Oh? Who was it, do you know?"

Brand shook his head. "Not even sure there *was* a babe. But that's usually why folks don't want the maid service and all."

The cottages were separate cabins, and Brand took me to Cottage 12. He knocked, but there wasn't any answer. "Don't think he's home," Brand told me. "Like I said, I haven't seen him around. Probably investigating somewhere—detective, you know."

"Yeah."

He looked at me in the glow of the flashlight he held. "Something the matter with you?"

"I'm all right." That sudden pain had caught me several times in the last half hour, but it was now subsiding to a dull ache that stayed with me, along with mild dizziness.

Mr. Brand opened the door, then pressed the light switch on the wall, saying, "I know you're a detective, but I still don't like to . . . Oh, my God!"

Looking past him, I could see the same thing Brand had seen. On our right was the open door to the bathroom, and halfway through it, sprawled on the floor, was a man's body.

I walked to the figure and touched the outflung hand. The arm moved easily, so there wasn't any rigor mortis. I guessed, though, that he'd been killed several days ago; rigor mortis could have set in and then left again, as it will after a few days. I could see the man's face, and it had the distinctively bluish tinge of cyanosis.

The dead man fit the description I had of Harry Welch; he had a lot of dark hair, gray at the temples, and a thin black mustache, but I asked Mr. Brand, "Would you say this is Welch?"

He came a couple steps forward and bent down, peering at the dead man's face, an expression of distaste on his own features. "Yes, but what happened to him? Look at that color; it's . . ." He made a grating sound deep in his throat.

"Cyanosis," I said. "One of the less important effects of cyanide poisoning. You'd better call the police."

Brand went out. I could see that the wrinkled collar of the white dress shirt the dead detective wore was open, and he wore no tie. He had on brown trousers and brown shoes.

It looked as if Welch had been relaxing at night after finishing a day's work. And he had almost surely been poisoned by somebody else. Suicide was such a remote possibility that I ignored it.

There wasn't anything to show that Welch hadn't been living here alone. I looked around for something he might have eaten or drunk from, but there wasn't anything like that in the cottage. In the dresser drawer, however, was the dead man's wallet. I flipped it open with a finger and examined the identification cards behind their transparent windows.

The dead man had been a private detective, all right, licensed by the state of California. His name was Harold M. Welch, and his address was in Fresno, California. So finally I knew where he'd come from.

Looking at the limp body on the floor, I wondered why Welch had been killed. There was one reason, or motive, that fit all facets of the case. But Welch, too, had been poisoned—with cyanide. And there had been cyanide in Ilona Cabot's milk.

I stopped. Remembering, I could hear Johnny Cabot saying to me at the Westlander Theater: "If I wanted to kill anybody, I wouldn't use cyanide, I'd use a gun." How had he known that the would-be murderer of his wife had used cyanide?

I thought about that, and when I remembered that Ilona had been gone by the time I'd arrived at the house on Robard Street, I felt sure I had the answer to that question—and more, including why Welch had been murdered, why there'd been the attempt on Ilona Cabot's life—in fact the whole story, including where Johnny Cabot and his three Ilonas fit in. But I still needed a little more information and a little more proof. And the place to get it was in my apartment, and the method was using the phone to call Fresno.

Carol Austin was still waiting for me in my apartment when I got there. I'd anticipated that, and would have been enormously surprised if she hadn't waited for my return. She didn't say anything when I walked in the door, just stared at me.

"Hi," I said. "I wondered if you'd still be here."

Only then did she smile and seem to relax. "You must have known I'd wait. What have you been doing?" Her blue eyes got very wide. "What happened to your clothes? It isn't raining, is it?"

I walked to the divan and sat down, reached for the phone. "No, I fell into a tank of water." She asked some more questions, but instead of answering them I dialed information and asked for the phone number of Mr. William Grant in Fresno.

Carol got up and said, "I'll mix us something to drink."

"Fine," I told her. "I'd like that."

While she moved about in the kitchenette, I listened to the operator getting in touch with Fresno, then asking for the number of William Grant.

Finally a woman's sleep-dulled voice was saying to me, "Hello."

"Hello, this is Shell Scott in Los Angeles. I wasn't sure I'd reach anyone at this number."

Carol came back and sat on the divan and handed me a dark-brown highball. "Bourbon and water, isn't it?" she whispered.

I nodded. At the other end of the line the woman was saying, "Mr. Grant passed away recently. Perhaps I can help you—I was his personal secretary for many years. I'm Joan Bates."

"What can you tell me about Mr. Harry Welch, a detective."

"Oh?" She hesitated. "I don't feel I should—"

"He's dead," I interrupted. "He was murdered. I'm an investigator, myself." I added, with only slight exaggeration, "I'm working quite closely with the police on this."

And that loosened her tongue. "I see— He's *dead,* then. We hadn't heard anything for several days. How awful! Are you sure he was murdered?"

"There's not any doubt. What can you tell me about him?"

"Well, he was working for the estate. When Mr. Grant's will was read, we learned that he'd left half of all his money to me and his nurse Ann Wilson, and the other half to a friend. But nobody knew where the—friend was living."

"You're referring to his daughter, aren't you?"

She gasped. "Why, how did you—"

"I know all about that, ma'am. Will you excuse me a minute?"

She said she'd hold the line, and I put the phone down on the cushion, then got to my feet, highball in my hand. "Any ice left?" I asked Carol. Or, at least, the lovely I thought of as Carol.

"Yes. Yes, lots. A tray's in the sink. What—"

She started to get up, but I said genially, "Relax, honey. I can do some of the work."

10. IN THE KITCHENETTE, out of sight of my guest,
I made noise getting the ice, rattling the tray
in the sink, while I held the highball close to
my nose and sniffed. It was obvious, once I looked for
it—or smelled for it. The peach-pit odor of potassium
cyanide rose even above the strong fumes of bourbon.
I poured the drink into the sink, quickly and quietly rinsed
my glass and filled it with tap water, plus enough Coca
Cola to give it a dark bourbon color, then added a couple
more ice cubes and went back into the front room.

Carol hadn't moved. She seemed almost rigid. I beamed
at her and said, "I like lots of ice. This conversation may
take quite a while." I sat down and picked up the phone,
holding my hand over the mouthpiece, then had a sizable
gulp of my water-and-Coke. "That's better," I said happily,
and then frowned, making a face. "But that's the bitterest
bourbon I ever tasted. Carol, next time use the Old Crow
—not that cheap stuff."

She nodded silently and smiled. It was a ghastly smile.
An hour earlier, I would probably have thought it charming, hot, lovable. But now I could see what it really was,
just muscles pulling at lips and cheeks.

Into the phone I said, "Hello again. Would you give
me the whole story, please?" She did.

While talking to the woman in Fresno, I sipped oc-
casionally at my drink. When she finished, I thanked her
and said I'd get in touch with her again the following
day, and hung up.

Carol Austin had her big blue eyes fastened on me
like blued steel to a magnet. She couldn't have learned
much from the phone conversation, because for the
most part I'd been listening, but she said, "Are you
getting your case all finished up, Shell?"

"Looks like it."

She raised her highball. "Relax a little. You'll live
longer. Bottoms up?"

Live longer, hey? "Bottoms up," I said, and drank the
rest of my Coke-and-water. It was fascinating to watch
Carol watch me. She didn't even seem to be breathing.
I said, "Would you like to hear about the case, honey?
About my fascinating life?"

She shrugged, as if that would be as good a way to kill
the next minute or two as any. I said, "Some of this I'd

already learned, and some of it I got on the phone from Fresno. I was talking to Fresno just now, did you know that?"

"I . . . thought maybe . . ." She stopped. "I mean, I don't know where it was."

"Well, it was Fresno. It seems a man named William J. Grant died up there a little while back, and this Mr. Grant had raked together about four million dollars. About twenty-two years ago, Mr. Grant and a girl named Mary Lassen were, well, let's say in love. Is this interesting to you?"

She gave me one of those pulled-muscle smiles again, as if she had just sprained her face. Carol knew something was very wrong, but she didn't seem sure exactly what it was. Then, too, I was dying rather slowly.

I said, "Well, to boil it down, they had a baby. And they weren't married. The old story; it's happened before, it'll happen again." And right there I stopped. I let what I fondly hoped was a stricken look capture my features. I waggled my face around and bent forward, saying harshly, "Arrggh!"

Carol didn't move an eighth of an inch. She stared at me, and in a voice completely devoid of surprise or even friendly curiosity, asked "What's the matter, Shell?"

"I— A pain. Feel a little dizzy. Something I . . ." After another groan or two I straightened up and shook my head. This time when I looked at Carol there was, oddly enough, an apparently real smile on her face. It was a small, hardly perceptible smile, but after all there wasn't much to laugh about.

"That was strange," I said, and went on. "Well, this guy Grant took a powder, left the Lassen woman and the child in the lurch. The woman turned the kid over to an orphanage and knocked herself off, and by the time Grant learned about that a year or so had passed. He didn't do anything about it. But after another twenty years, he took real sick. He was dying, and his thoughts turned to the girl—his daughter. He was a rich man by then, and he wanted half his fortune to go to the girl. Is this boring you, Carol?"

"What? Oh, no, Shell. This is interesting."

"Fine. There's not much more. I—arrgh!"

I did it all again. Carol really seemed to enjoy this

spasm and kept looking at me hopefully. But I recovered and continued, although in a weak voice.

"Well, Grant died, and the executors of the estate, in accordance with his wishes, hired a detective named Welch to find the missing daughter. All they could tell the detective was the name of the orphans' home, and the date the girl had been left there by her mother. Welch checked the home and learned the girl had been named Ilona. So he started hunting up gals named Ilona."

"Ilona?" Carol said gently. "Isn't that odd?"

"The odd part is that you asked me about Ilona Cabot earlier. And I didn't ever tell you that the homely Ilona in my office was named Cabot. I did foolishly admit to you this morning that I was looking for her husband; and you must have heard me talking to Missing Persons on the phone about a missing John *Cabot*. I mean when you came into my office with that spur-of-the-moment story about thinking it was Dr. Forrest's. I suppose you put one and one together and tonight asked me about Ilona Cabot to make sure that was, in fact, her married name."

Carol didn't say anything. I went on, "Well, to continue, nobody around the late Mr. Grant even knew he had a daughter until the will was read. That's understandable, under the circumstances. Anyway, all his money was left to just three people. Two of them in Fresno—Grant's personal secretary, and his private nurse, both of whom had been with him for years. He had no other relatives, so half his estate went to those two. The other half was to go to his daughter. And that, of course, set up a kind of dangerous situation for this Ilona."

"Oh? I—don't understand," said Carol.

What she probably didn't understand was why I was still able to yak away, but I went on, "Nobody knew for sure if this Ilona was still alive. If found, she would inherit a couple million dollars. But if nobody found her— or if she were dead—according to the terms of the will the two million would then devolve upon the secretary and nurse. That's an extra million bucks apiece. There's a nice motive for murder—murder for a million. So it looks as if either Grant's secretary or his nurse tried to knock off Ilona. It's really too bad what the hunger for money will do to otherwise nice people."

Carol was looking at me strangely, in apparent puzzlement. I hadn't gasped and gurgled for quite a while, and probably she felt that I was taking a distressingly long time to die. So I went into my dying-horribly act.

Suddenly I gasped twice as loud and gurgled much more musically then anything I'd achieved yet. I sprang to my feet and straightened up, then bent forward like a man doing a jackknife, arms going around my stomach. I spun about, staggering, toppled forward almost at Carol's feet, and continued groaning while writhing on the carpet.

Carol didn't extend a helping hand, didn't say a word, didn't do a thing. In momentary glimpses that I got of her from my rolling eyes, I saw that she had merely put her arms across her breasts, hands clasping her shoulders, and was gently hugging herself. Her narrowed blue eyes were fixed on me, and that tight little smile twisted her soft red lips.

Finally I got to my hands and knees and raised my face so I could stare at her. "You!" I croaked. "You've croaked me!"

Her eyes were bright. She squinted at me, pressing against the divan as if to move farther from me. I said, "It was you, Carol. You killed Welch—and tried twice to kill Ilona."

She got to her feet and started to step around me. This wasn't the way I'd planned it. So, in what must have appeared my final burst of living, I struggled to my feet and staggered toward Carol.

Her eyes widened, a little fright showing in them at last. Because she must have thought I would by now be unable to move with much grace or speed, she spun around to run, too late. I jumped about six feet through the air and grabbed her, turned her to face me, and mashed her tightly against me. "Tell me the truth!" I shouted as we both toppled to the floor.

Her face was only about three inches from mine, and she really looked frightened now. "Yes," she half whimpered. "I did kill him. I couldn't let him tell where she was. And I tried to kill her—but I didn't, I didn't kill her. Let me go. Let me go!"

I just squeezed her tighter. We were lying on our sides on the thick shag nap of my carpet, and I couldn't very well have been holding her more tightly. Her breasts mashed against me, her thighs pressed mine, and she was after all a very delightfully fashioned female. She was moving a lot, too. And I wasn't really dying. In fact, I was living.

I said, "You tried to kill her with a car last Sunday, and then by lacing her milk with cyanide this morning. Didn't you?"

"Yes, yes!"

"And you were much surprised when Ilona came out of her house alive. So you followed her to my office this morning, right, love?"

She nodded. All of this wallowing about had sort of upped my blood pressure. After those last two words, Carol hadn't said anything else, but every second she was straining against me, moving frantically, squirming and trying to get away, and it was almost enough all by itself to kill a man. I'm only human. Pretty quick I even forgot what questions I'd been meaning to ask this gal.

And, inevitably, Carol finally got my message. Her face went through a startling array of expressions. First, a queer kind of amazement. A sort of "Can this be?" look, as though it were too soon for rigor mortis to be setting in. And then the expression of a person slowly, and with complete awareness of what was happening, experiencing apoplexy. And then, at last, Carol's much-used sexy look.

She had me pegged. Hell, I had her pegged, too. But she knew what old Shell Scott was interested in. She knew, all right. And she figured, I guess, that she could take advantage of my interest in hers. At any rate, she began speaking to me, softly.

"What if I did kill that detective, Shell? What difference does it make, really? We can have a lot of fun together, you and I. I'll be rich, Shell, rich. Millions, millions of dollars. For both of us . . ."

She was still squirming, wriggling around there on the carpet. But she wasn't trying to get away. "Once Ilona's taken care of," she said, "I'll have two million dollars—maybe even more later. We'll have to get rid of her husband, too. I didn't even know until this morning that she was married." She paused. "Shell, if we can get rid of both of them, there'll maybe be four million later. That's more money than I can imagine—but it was supposed all to be mine. Bill said once that it would all be mine."

For a second or two that "Bill" puzzled me, but then I

realized she must have referred to Grant, William Grant
as I knew him. Maybe she and Bill had played games
on carpets, or had some less unusual arrangement. Carol's
face wasn't frightened any longer, it was only an inch
or two from mine, and she was smiling again. The smile,
though, was still that pulled-muscle operation. She looked
not quite all there, as if mentally she were absent, or at
least tardy.

She went on, speaking softly, "I know you like me. I
can tell when a man likes me."

"Welch, for example? He must have liked you pretty
well. You were living with him at those Rancho cottages,
weren't you?

"For a little while, but I had to be close to him so I'd
know when he found Ilona. If he found her."

"He didn't know you were Ann Wilson, did he?" I held
my breath, but she answered without any hesitation.

"Of course not. I made up a name for him. I managed
to meet him in a bar. It's a good thing. He'd even written
up his report before he told me he'd finished what he'd
been hired to do. That he'd found the girl he was looking
for. After I—after he died, I burned the report. That's
how I learned where Ilona was."

"And were you the one who shot at me earlier tonight?"

"Shot at you? I don't know what you're talking about."

I believed her. She was quiet for seconds, then she put
her cheek against mine and said, in a pleased voice that
was almost laughing, "You do like me a lot, I know. And
we will have fun together, won't we? You won't tell anybody about me, will you, Shell?"

"Baby, we are off to the clink."

It didn't penetrate for a few moments. Then she pulled
back her head and stared at me. "What? What did you
say?"

"Honey, that second drink you made me earlier—the
one you mixed all by yourself in the kitchenette—had
enough poison in it to kill me for sure. I was just another
Welch who might upset your plans. Luckily I had only a
small sip of the drink, but even so, it affected me a little
after I'd left here. I just can't afford to do any more
drinking with you, sweet. You must have brought eight
pounds of cyanide down here from Fresno."

"Oh, you're imagining things, Shell." Yeah, she was

nuts, all right. "I wouldn't do anything to hurt you." Man, she was squirming and wobbling around like crazy.

"No, of course not," I said pleasantly. "I didn't realize quite what was wrong until I saw Welch's body, and the blue tinge of cyanosis on his face. That told me what was wrong with me, my love, and who was responsible for it all. That was the dead giveaway. No, love, I'm afraid I'll have to take you to jail."

And this time she believed me. She hauled off and hit me with everything she had—that is, everything she hadn't already hit me with. Arms, elbows, head, knees and so on. She even tried to bite me. I finally had to tie her arms and legs with electrical cord from one of the living-room lamps.

11.

THE POLICE had taken Ann Wilson, alias Carol Austin, away from my apartment an hour before, and I was just knocking at the door of apartment 12 in the Franklin. While waiting for the police to arrive, the Franklin's desk clerk had phoned to earn his twenty bucks, and report the arrival of Cabot and his wife. So I had come straight here as soon as I could; this would wrap the case up. But I hated the thought of what the truth was going to do to Ilona. Johnny wasn't going to be happy, either, so I took out my .38 Colt and held it in my hand as I waited.

Footsteps sounded inside, then the door opened part way. Johnny Cabot blinked sleepily at me and began to speak. But then his eyes snapped open, he started to slam the door as a swear word burst from his throat.

"Hold it, Cabot!" I shoved the gun toward his sharp nose, and he froze. He stared at the gun, inches from his face, and I said, "Ask me in, Cabot. The party's over."

"What the hell's the idea? I've had about—"

"Shut up. You going to ask me in?"

He glanced again at my coat pocket, then stepped back. I walked in and looked around. The door into the next room, the bedroom, was ajar. From the bedroom Ilona's voice called, "What is it, Johnny?"

"I'll—be right in," he said, then looked at me.

I spoke softly, "Get her and bring her out here, Cabot. I'll do this much for you, though I don't know why—you can tell her if you want to; or I will. You can have your choice."

He licked his lips. "Tell her what?"

"Come off it. You're washed up. I know all about William Grant, your bride's inheritance, the works."

He sighed, then shrugged. "Well," he said finally, "you can't blame me for trying. You—uh, you better tell her, Scott. She is pretty much of a mess, but—well, I don't want to tell her."

"I didn't think anything would bother you, Cabot." He shrugged, and I said, "Tell her to come out. But you keep in my sight. I'd hate for you to come back with that forty-five in your mitt."

"What forty-five?"

"The one you shot at me with earlier tonight."

He started to deny it, but then walked to the door and told Ilona to put on some clothes and come out. Then he shut the door, walked over and said to me, "I guess there's no point in trying to make it work now. Sure, I shot at you—or at your car. Don't kid yourself, mister. If I'd wanted to plug you, I wouldn't have missed by three or four feet. I just wanted to scare you off me and Ilona." He paused. "Maybe I should have shot you—but I'm not a murderer."

This time I believed him. I put the .38 in my coat pocket but kept my hand on it and said, "I figured you were for a while, Cabot. I found Welch's body tonight—"

"He's dead?" Honest surprise was in his voice.

"Several days. Poisoned. I thought you might have done it, but under the circumstance you'd have been nuts to kill him. You wanted him alive—at least long enough to report to Fresno that he'd found Ilona. But because you'd told me at the Westlander you wouldn't use cyanide to kill somebody, I figured you must've slipped the cyanide into your wife's milk."

"You're way off," he said. "The minute after you talked to me at the Westlander I called Ilona, asked her what the score was. She told me about bringing the milk to your office, cyanide and all. She told me."

"Uh-huh. That's the way it figured to me."

"Welch's been dead several days? You mean they don't know Ilona's here in L.A." He grinned wryly. "Not that it makes any difference to *me* now."

He was almost likeable for a second there. Cabot talked freely enough, now that he knew the game was over.

As I had guessed, he'd first talked to Welch on the 15th when the detective came into the Westlander Theater to check on Ilona the Hungarian Hurricane. Cabot had learned enough from Ilona and Welch himself that he stuck to Welch like a leech. They'd visited the Grotto, where Welch had interviewed Neptuna—and Cabot had got an eyeful that almost knocked him off his feet.

He and Welch had planned to have dinner the next night, but Welch had phoned to say he'd found the girl he was looking for and thus couldn't make it.

I said, "How much did Welch tell you? Did he actually say the Ilona he'd found was going to inherit a couple million? Did he tell you where she lived?"

Cabot shrugged. "No, he just said she was going to get some money from the estate of a guy named William J. Grant—he didn't tell Ilona that; his job was only to find her. I knew Welch was from Fresno, checked recent Fresno papers and learned this Grant had been loaded. The next day when Welch phoned me, I asked him where he'd found the girl and he said in an insurance office on Hill. I didn't ask him to narrow it down. The rest of it was just a little checking here and with Fresno." He shrugged again. "A couple million bucks was worth a good try."

"What I can't understand is why you took off Monday night and didn't come back."

"Well, you've seen my . . . wife. And you've seen Ilona Betun. I thought I could get away with it."

That was a good enough answer. Cabot told me that he'd kept his job at the burlesque house because he wasn't supposed to know his Ilona was going to inherit any money, and it would later have looked funny if he had quit his job as soon as they'd met. Besides, he added dully, they really did need the money.

The door opened then and Ilona Cabot came in. Wearing her husband's robe, and with no makeup, her hair almost straight, she didn't look good at all. Not pretty, at least. She still had that air of mousy sweetness about her.

Her face brightened with a smile when she saw me. "Mr. Scott. What are you doing here?"

"Hello, Mrs. Cabot. You'd better sit down."

We all found seats, me in a chair and Ilona with Johnny on the couch. She grabbed his hand and held it. Johnny was starting to look very uncomfortable.

Just to be positive, I asked her if she'd spent the first half dozen years of her life in the Bunting Orphanage, and if a detective named Welch had talked to her a couple weeks ago about that. After a little hesitation she admitted it, but expressed her puzzlement.

I said, "Well, Mrs. Cabot, you're an heiress. I mean, you'll soon inherit about two million dollars."

It went right by her. If I was talking about two million dollars, I couldn't possibly be talking about her. It took me five minutes to partially convince her that she was actually going to get money, and explain enough so she could believe it. When she finally got it through her head, all she did was turn to Cabot and say, "Johnny, isn't it wonderful?"

I broke in quickly, "Wait a minute. That's not all of what I've got to tell you. The other part is about your husband. About Johnny."

She smiled. "Yes?" She looked at Johnny Cabot. She beamed at him.

I remembered how she had lit up in my office when I'd asked her to describe her husband. This was the same kind of look. A bright, happy, everything's-wonderful look. It wasn't a very new expression, not original, just the look of a woman in love.

But it was, of course, new for Ilona.

I hated to think of how she was going to look when she knew that Johnny Cabot had found out about her from Welch, learned from Welch about her inheritance, found her and rushed her and married her, just for whatever part he could grab of that two million bucks. I didn't like the thought of what was going to happen to her already plain and homely face.

I said, "You see, Mrs. Cabot, this detective, Welch, who talked to you—well, he talked to some other Ilonas first, before he found you. During his search for you. Two million dollars is an awful lot of money, and . . ." I stopped. It was difficult to find the right words. It was going to hurt enough no matter how it was told, but I wanted to find the gentlest way to break it to her, if I could.

But then Cabot said slowly, "Let it go, Scott. This is something I . . . Well, maybe I better tell her." He chewed on his lip for a moment, then turned to her. "Honey, it's like this. When I met you, I—well, I—"

Ilona was looking up at him, sort of smiling. And it seemed to me that she didn't look plain and almost ugly —not when she was looking at her husband. Her face seemed to get bright and warm, as if it were lighted from happiness welling up inside her, and I thought that all the hunger and trampled-down love and affection she must have been saving for years was right there on her face. It was there in the brightness of her eyes, and in the curve of her lips. It was so frank and honest and open that it didn't seem quite right for me to be looking at her then.

Johnny had taken a deep breath, and now he said, rapidly, not looking at her, "Honey, when I met you I told you I was crazy about you, you remember, but the real reason I bumped into you was because I knew all about—"

"Wait a minute. Hold it, just a minute."

I was on my feet and the words had popped out of me almost involuntarily. All I knew was that I didn't want to see Ilona's face change from the expression it now wore to one of hurt and disillusionment. Or maybe I was just out of my mind.

But, anyway, I went on in a rush, "I can't sit around here all night listening to you two gab away. This is probably the same thing your husband said to me just a little while ago when I told him about the money you're inheriting. He said he was afraid you might not feel the same toward him, now that you're a millionaire."

"Johnny!" she cried. She was shocked.

I went on, "What I wanted to tell you about was the other half of the job you hired me for. Somebody really was trying to kill you, Mrs. Cabot. It was a woman named Ann Wilson. She was scheduled to inherit a million herself, but that wasn't enough for her, so she tried to knock you off. I think she's a little cracked—anyway, the cops have her in the hoosegow now, so all your troubles are over. Funny, you'll probably inherit half of the million she would have gotten."

"All my troubles are over," she said softly. "I just can't understand it—all this at once."

Neither could Cabot. He was gaping at me, his mouth half open. I walked to the door and out into the hall, then I jerked my head at him. "I'd like to have a last word with you, Cabot."

He came outside and shut the door. "What the hell?" he said, bewildered. "What happened just now?"

"I had a cerebral hemorrhage. Shut up and listen. That little girl in there must be crazier than Ann Wilson, because she thinks you're the end. Well, I think you're the other end, but maybe you could be real nice to this Ilona-with-two-million-dollars, if you tried. And I've got a hunch you're going to try."

He nodded slowly. "Yeah. You're making sense." He paused. "I didn't think you were flipping your lid in there for me."

I said, "I can still tell her, you know. I can still prove it. I'd hate to tear apart two people so much in love, though."

"You know," he said quietly, "she's really prettier now than when I met her. Not pretty—but less horrible."

"Wait'll she gets that inheritance. She'll be beautiful."

I was being sarcastic, in a way, but somehow I had a hunch that Ilona—with a lot more love, and a little more money—just might work her way up to not-half-bad. Well, time would tell.

I nodded at Johnny Cabot and said, "Tell your wife I'll be sending her a bill for my fee. My *big* fee."

I walked down the hall. Before I reached the elevator I heard the door shut behind me. When I looked around, the door was closed and Johnny Cabot was again alone with his wife. . . .

Because I kept wondering about Johnny and his Ilona even after I got in the Cad and started home, I was well out Beverly Boulevard and actually passing the Grotto before I remembered the other Ilona. Neptuna. *My* Ilona.

I slammed on the breaks so suddenly that the car skidded to a stop in the middle of the street. A quick glance at the dash clock showed me it was three A.M. What was it Ilona Betun had said? She'd asked me to come back if I could, and said she would wait around a little while after closing. After two A.M. Well, it was only an hour after two. Maybe she'd still be here.

I swung into the parking lot, parked the car and trotted to the club's rear entrance. With mild surprise I discovered that I was grinning. My Ilona had also said, I remembered, that sometimes she had a little swim all by herself here after everybody else had gone.

I paused before the Grotto's rear door to catch my breath, then put my hand on the knob. It turned easily and the door opened. Inside, the club was dark. I could see nothing but blackness beyond the door. But the fact that this door had been unlocked was encouraging, I thought.

Either the club was being burglarized, or Ilona was waiting. I went in, shut the door behind me, and walked ahead, still grinning, through the darkness.

❖❖❖❖❖❖❖❖❖❖❖❖❖❖

Hot-Rock
Rumble

SOMEHOW Mr. Osborne didn't look like the type. He was a tall, distinguished-looking guy of about fifty, with all his hair still on his head, rimless glasses over his blue eyes, and about three hundred dollars' worth of clothes on his short body.

He'd come in through the door marked "Sheldon Scott, Investigations" at ten this morning and he'd given me his whole story in five minutes, his sentences clipped and to the point. About every minute he'd gone to the window that overlooks Broadway and peered out to see if his wife were standing down there screeching.

I said, "Sounds okay. I'll get on it right away, Mr. Osborne."

"Thank you." He got up, found a thousand-dollar bill in his fat wallet and dropped the bill on my desk. "I hope that's all right for now. I'll give you the other nine thousand in cash too, if you're successful. Is that satisfactory?" He went over to the window again.

"Perfectly." I was admiring Cleveland's picture and the number one and three zeros in the bill's corner when he said, "Ohmigawd. There she is. She didn't shop long. She can spend more money faster than anybody I . . ." He let it trail off, turned and went sailing out without another word.

In his haste he left my office door standing open. I shut it, then walked to the window where he'd been standing. I saw him appear beside a plump woman in a fur coat. She put her hands on her hips and yakked something at him.

It seemed likely she was asking him where in the hell he'd disappeared to, because Mr. Jules Osborne had sneaked away from his wife to see me. I went back to my desk and looked at the notes I'd taken while he'd talked. Mr. Osborne had spent $100,000 on jewelry which, unknown to his wife, he had given to what he described as "an, ah, er, young lady." Two nights ago the jewelry had been stolen from the girl's—Diane Borden's—home. Diane missed her rocks so much that she brought forth an ultimatum: if Julie boy didn't replace them, or at least get the "old" ones back, Mrs. Jules Osborne might start hearing from the little birds. So, with a possible outlay of $100,000 staring him in the wallet, Jules was quite willing to pay me $10,000 if I could recover the originals.

Osborne hadn't gone to the police because he didn't want any record of this deal anywhere. He'd checked on me, satisfied himself I could be trusted, and laid his problem in my lap. And time was important because he'd said to me, "I can trust the jeweler, I'm sure. The only one I'm worried about is Diane. She's apt to go berserk any day. Any—" he groaned— "hour. If my wife finds out about this she'll gouge me for a million-a-year alimony. What with alimony and taxes I'll have to borrow money."

Anyway, Osborne wanted action. Diane lived in a rent-free house on Genesee Street. I put the thousand bucks in my wallet, got my black Cad out of the parking lot, and headed for Hollywood.

2. As soon as I saw Diane I knew she must have given Jules his hundred-thousand-dollars' worth. There were several things about Diane that were obvious, the first one being that she was a woman. A lot of women these days look like thin men, but not this kid. She was dressed in red-and-black hostess pajamas with a silver belt tied around her tiny waist. The pajama bottoms were the black part, with full flowing legs slit up the side to her knees—which I automatically assumed were dimpled—and the red part was a thin, shimmering blouse which was crammed either with gigantic falsies or one hell of a lot of Diane.

She peered around the door and up at me, letting a strand of red hair droop fetchingly over one eye, and she said, "Hello, hello, hello."

I looked behind me but there was nobody else around. "That all for me?" I asked her.

"Sure. You're big enough for three hellos. You're Scotty, aren't you?"

"Shell Scott. How did you know?"

"Daddy phoned me. He said you'd come around and see me." She had the door about halfway open and she slid around it, one arm and leg on each side of it and her body pressed against the thin edge. She was silent for a few seconds, smiling at me, then she said, "He told me you were big, and your nose was a little bent, and you had real short white hair that stuck up in the air, and I should be nice to you and help you any way I could." She laughed. "Come on in, Mr. Scotty. I'm Diane."

There was a chance conversation with this gal was going to be difficult. I walked by her but before I got past she said, "He didn't tell me about the funny white eyebrows. They glued?" She reached out and playfully tugged at one.

"No," I said. "They are not glued. And I—"

"You bring my jewels?"

"What the hell—"

"I know you didn't. I was just teasing. Don't be mad. Come in and sit down. You want a drink or anything?"

"Nope. I want some conversation. You sit down in a chair clear the hell across the room from me and let's talk. Okay?"

She pretended to pout, which let me notice how full and sensually curving her lower lip was. While I sat down she plopped into a chair and crossed her legs. That black cloth parted at the slit and fell away from skin that looked white and soft as a cloud. Then she bounced up and sat on a long gray divan for half a second, then rolled over and lay on her stomach looking at me. She was a fluffy little bit of a thing, very young—maybe seventeen, I figured, all curves and bounce and energy. She was beginning to make me feel decrepit and full of hardened arteries at thirty.

Finally we got around to the jewelry. On my way here I'd stopped at Montclair Jewelers, where Osborne had bought the stuff, and picked up a typed list and description of the missing items. Osborne had arranged to have it ready for me. The pieces were mostly diamonds, with a couple of emerald brooches thrown in. I checked the list against Diane's memory, which was just as good as the list, then asked her to tell me what she could of the actual theft.

She rolled over onto her back, stretched her arms above her head, and presented such a charming picture that I hardly heard what she was saying. But she told me she'd gone with "Daddy" to an out-of-the-way spot and worn some of her diamonds. Back home, after Mr. Osborne had gone, she'd left the stuff on top of her bedroom dresser alongside the jewel box.

She said, "And when I woke up yesterday morning the little pretties were just gone. I'd locked the doors when Daddy left and they were still locked this morning. Windows too. But it was all just gone. Some robbers stole it all."

"You mean somebody walked right into your bedroom and lifted the rocks without your knowing anything about it?"

"Well, they must have. I sleep soundly enough, but if anybody was banging around and flashing lights and things it should have awakened me." She giggled at me. "I wasn't very tired, anyway."

"Yeah. You know, I expected to find you all broken up, yanking your hair out and wailing. You sure you want these things back?"

"Well, I like that. You want me to run around bawling and yelling 'My jewels, my jewels'?" She was still smiling and didn't seem angry. "Now, wouldn't that be silly, really? I really feel bad, but Daddy said you'd get them back . . . or else he'd get me some more. So it's not as if my little old pretties were gone forever."

"I was just thinking, wouldn't it be a big laugh if you still had those little old pretties around somewhere and I naturally can't find the robbers and you get another hundred grand's worth from Da—ah, from your father?"

She sat up straight on the couch. "Let me think about that a minute," she said. Then she laughed, flopped back on the couch and threw her legs up in the air. "Oh, how funny," she said. "That *would* be a scream. But I never thought of it—wish I had. And he's not my father, you silly. You know what I hope?"

"No, what do you hope?"

"That those robbers didn't see me." She swung her legs around to the floor, got up and scooted across the room and curled up on the floor at my feet. She put her arms on my knees, leaned forward and said, "If they saw the diamonds, right in my bedroom there, and stole them, they must have been able to see me, it seems like. And golly I hope they didn't. I sleep without anything on, nothing at all, you know, and I'm restless. I kick and turn and wallow around all night I guess. Almost always I wake up all uncovered." She shook her head and let red hair fly around.

I said in a voice that was practically normal, "And if those robbers did see you, you'd better lock and bar all the doors tonight, because they'll be here again come hell or high water, jewels or no jewels. Now go back to your couch."

She laughed and said, "You're fun. You know, you're lots of fun. And you know what I meant. Well, what else do you want to know?"

"You got any picture of you wearing some of the rocks?"

"Just a minute." She got up, taking her arms and what-not off my shaking knees, and trotted out of the room on bare feet. I hadn't noticed before that she was bare-footed, but then I've never been much of a guy to look at feet.

She came back with two snapshots and a nightclub photo in which she was practically sagging under the weight of diamonds and emeralds. The nightclub photo showed a necklace, pin, and bracelet clearly. The dress she'd been wearing was strapless, and the photo showed Diane clearly, and it was clearly all Diane.

"You can borrow the pictures," she said. "Daddy took the first two snaps, and he was in the other—but he cut himself out. Well, what now?"

"Now I go look for these things. And I'd be awfully sad if there weren't any robbers."

"There you go again. Don't be so nasty. Somebody stole them, all right. You have to go right away?"

"Immediately." I stood up. I looked at her for a minute and said, "Aren't you being a little rough on the guy? I mean this business of either you get the rocks back or it costs him another hundred G's? The guy might collapse from anxiety, start selling his Cadillacs, get rocks in his head—"

"Wait a minute." She raised an arched eyebrow and looked me up and down slowly. Then she said, "Come on now. You know better than that. I'm doing him a favor. A lot of men think price is value. Daddy wouldn't have a Cadillac if it cost only five hundred dollars."

I blinked at her, thinking that maybe her brain wasn't

as soft as I'd suspected. Then she went back to normal and wiggled a little and smiled at me, and I thought: Hang on, Scott, you'll be out of here in a minute and Jules isn't paying you for what you're thinking. I started for the door and Diane walked along with me, hanging onto my arm, which also started getting hot.

"If you find them," she said, "you bring them back to me. Don't take them to Daddy. They're mine."

"Don't worry. I'm not supposed to go within a mile of him. I'll bring them to you—if I find them."

She opened the door and slid around it again in that oddly interesting fashion. "All right," she said smiling, "just you don't sneak in at night like they did, and leave them on the dresser."

I grinned. "If I do, I'll look the other way."

"Sure," she said. "Away from the dresser." She giggled. "I bet you make lots of money."

"Not that much. And it all goes in taxes. Well, goodby, Miss Borden."

" 'Bye, Mr. Scotty."

I went out onto the porch and just before she shut the door she said, "Don't call me Miss Borden." I looked over my shoulder at her and she said, "Call me Diane." She took one arm off the door and kind of waved it at me, letting her hand fall limp from her wrist, then winked at me and said, "And listen, you. I'm older than I look."

Then she shut the door and I thought about sitting down on the grass and rolling around howling, and I thought about jumping up and running back and crashing through the door, but what I did was go out to the Cad and lean my head against the cool steering wheel for a couple seconds, then shiver spasmodically and put the buggy in gear thinking that Jules Osborne should have told me more about Diane, and offered me at least twenty thousand dollars.

3.

AT THE OFFICE I reviewed what little I knew and phoned Burglary Division in City Hall to refresh my memory. Then I propped my cordovans on the desk and thought for a couple of minutes. Starting about three months back, there had been a number of night burglaries in and near Los Angeles, ranging from Beverly Hills to Boyle Heights. This particular rash of burglaries totaled nine reported so far; the m.o. was the same in all of them and unlike any known gang which Burglary had any record of. The capers always came off between ten at night and two in the morning, there was never any sign that doors or windows had been forced. Nobody had ever reported any lights in the burgled houses, though some of the jobs had been pulled off next door to houses in which parties were going on or in which the occupants were chatting or watching television. The doors were always still locked when the people got home to find their jewels, money, furs, silver gone. The jobs had been well cased and the hauls were always good ones, the loot taken from wealthy people. The burglars had never been seen or heard, and Burglary didn't have a solitary lead.

Homicide was interested too, because on one job, which both Burglary and Homicide agreed was obviously the work of the same ten-to-two gang, a wealthy attorney named William Drake had been murdered. And in messy fashion. It was assumed that he'd left his wife at a party and come home alone while the gang was in his big house on San Vicente Boulevard—the coroner set the time of death at around midnight—and the attorney had been brutally beaten by what must have been an exceedingly powerful man. The attorney's face was a pulp, and one blow had broken his neck. He'd also been shot, a bullet from a .45 blowing away much of his brain.

Three of the jobs had been in the section between Wilshire Boulevard and Pico, the area in which Diane Borden lived, and there was a fair chance that Diane's pretties had been number five. The m.o. seemed the same in every particular.

I took my feet off the desk and made half a dozen more phone calls, then left the office and talked to a shoe-shine boy, two cab drivers, a bookie's runner, a bartender, and a barber. With several lines out I went back to the office and waited for a bite.

A lot of any private detective's time is spent in waiting, and more cases are broken with phones than with guns. At the core of any investigator's success, whether he's police or private, are his sources of information—the informers, stoolies, canaries. That's the unofficial staff. Over the years in Los Angeles I'd built up a long list of them and many of them were now, I hoped, out work-

ing for me—or might, already, know something that
would help. I'd dropped several words in several places,
and sent out a thumbnail description of some of the
most distinctive items I was interested in.

At three o'clock I got a nibble and, though I didn't
know it then, I landed a whale. The call was from an
alcoholic hoodlum with the unlikely name of Joseph Raspberry, and he wanted me to meet him in the back booth
of Manny's bar on Sixth. He also wanted me to bring
him a sawbuck. I told him to order a shot on me, that
I'd be there in ten minutes.

On my way over I wondered if he had anything. Joseph
Raspberry was a two-time loser who, when sober, was a
good thief. I'd picked him up a year ago and found him
carrying a gun, which isn't encouraged by parole boards
—and he was on parole at the time. I gave him a break,
which was illegal from the strictest point of view, but
which if enforced strictly would put all the cops and
private detectives in the clink. Since then Joe had stayed
out of stir and passed along a dozen tips to me, about
half of which paid off, and one of which helped me break
a murder case. The other tips were fakes, pure and simple,
and he dreamed them up because he wanted money for
his sweetheart, Old Crow-and-Coca Cola. I always gave
him ten or so, because there was always another time,
another tip. Then, too, when he wasn't hitting the pot
he was a likable character. I didn't know much about him,
and even the odd name might have been a fake or a
monicker. Anyway, I usually got a charge out of him; I
liked the guy for no good reason.

But this looked like one of the days when Joe needed
money for his sweetheart. He was huddled in the gloom
of a booth at the rear of Manny's, his thin face pinched,
hands shaking, lips twitching once in a while. I sat down
opposite him and he said, "Scott, Manny wouldn't gimme
a drink. An' I ain't got a bean."

"You had any breakfast, Joe?"

"Sure. Alka Seltzer and alcohol. Tell him it's okay, huh?"

I waved at Manny and he waddled over, wiping his
hands on a reasonably white apron. "A beer for me,
Manny," I said. "And a couple shots for Joe."

I always felt funny about buying a drink for Joe—or
any of the others like him. But if he didn't get it from

me he'd get it from somebody else, somehow. He was sick, but it wasn't my job to try healing all the sick people. When the shots arrived Joe started to lift one of them but his hand was shaking so much he knew he'd spill it. He put his fingers around the jigger, pressing his hand against the table, then bent forward and got his lips on the rim of the glass and sucked. He lifted the jigger then and tossed the whisky down. He didn't spill a drop.

I sipped my beer and waited. Finally he shuddered, pulled the other shot over in front of him and, looking at it, said, "I got something for you."

I put a ten-dollar bill in front of him. He licked his lips and said, "Gimme a pencil." I found a pencil stub in my pocket and gave it to him. He started drawing on a napkin. It took him three minutes, but he didn't touch the other shot till he'd finished. Then he lifted the glass, his hand not shaking so much this time, and tossed the drink off.

He pointed at the napkin. "Lupo seen me and says you been askin' for somethin' like that. If it's right, it's worth more'n a saw, ain't it?"

The drawing was crude: a bracelet with a lot of diamonds, and curving off from it a snake's head with the tongue licking out and two over-sized eyes in its head. It could have been something to get excited about, because crude as it was it looked like the bracelet Diane had been wearing in the nightclub photo. I had the picture in my pocket, but I didn't take it out yet. Joe just might have made his drawing from the description I'd sent around.

I said, "Could be," took a twenty-dollar bill from my wallet and wrapped it around my finger. He reached for it, but I said, "The story first, Joe. The ice looks right, maybe, but give me what you've got. And don't make any of it up, even if you haven't got much."

"Sure. I'll level with you, Scott." He hesitated. "I give you some bum ones, but this one's the McCoy. I seen it. Yesterday it was. It was on Wilcox, that's all I know for sure. I was . . . wasn't feelin' good."

That meant he'd been drunk. He licked his lips and looked at the empty shot glasses. I waved at Manny. And a minute later, over the filled glasses, with Joe's sharp whisky breath in my nostrils, I got fragments of a story from him, the rest of it still lost somewhere in his drunkard's brain. There wasn't any sound in the quiet of Manny's except Joe's voice, and as he talked I could almost see what had happened through Joe's eyes, everything out of shape, part of a different world with darker shadows and brighter sun, a strange and unreal and exaggerated world that Joe often lived in.

I could see him on the street, his throat aching for a drink, his body hungry for it. He stumbled in off the street into a bar and there was this guy. "He was a tall guy," Joe said. "Jesus, he was clear up to the ceiling, ten feet tall he was and he was stooped over by this booth thing, a kind of funny little booth thing there that had a doll in it. He give her the hoop and she put it on. I was right inside the door a little, next to the dumb thing she was in, and I seen it good. The eyes was red like the snake was alive on it, just like it was alive there." He talked in a monotone, slowly twirling the shot glass. "She took it and put it on and the big guy took it off of her, squeezin' her a little, and stuck it in her purse there. I was right up alongside them then; I thought she was at a bar but it wasn't no bar, and then the big guy seen me. He gimme a shove, for nothin', just shoved me back up on the wall and the whole place was goin' around. I tried to tell him I just wanted a drink and he picked me up and pushed me out. Like to ripped my head off."

"This guy, Joe. How big you say he was?"

"He was ten feet tall. Don't laugh; I'm not lyin'. He was at least twice as big as me, ten feet tall, clear up to the ceiling he was."

If it hadn't been for the crude drawing Joe had made I might have left then; if there were any truth in the story it seemed so distorted that it wouldn't help me. But I asked him, "What about the girl? What did she look like?"

"I dunno. But I seen her leave and I followed her."

"Why?"

He blinked at me and didn't answer for almost a minute. "I seen where she lived," he said finally.

That was enough, and it made sense to me. Joe was a good thief between cures, but when he needed a shot he'd steal anything from a baby carriage to a diamond bracelet. He went on, "I don't remember what she looked like, but she had a walk like nothing I ever seen. It was a circus, Scott."

"Where'd she go?"

"Right acrost from Polly's. Right on the corner. You know it?"

Polly's was a beer joint where you could place a bet in the back room. I knew the spot. "You're sure, Joe? You got this straight?"

"Yeah," he said. "It don't seem real, does it?" He licked his lips again. "But it's straight, Scott. I give it to you straight."

I took out the nightclub photo and showed it to him. "On the doll's wrist. That look near enough?"

He bent over the print, then looked up at me, a pleased expression on his face. "That's it. I swear that's it. But that ain't the doll. I'm pretty sure it ain't."

I gave him the twenty. "Got anything else to tell me, Joe?"

He shook his head and spread the money out before him on the table.

"Joe," I said, "give a listen. Why don't you spend some of that for a big steak? Get yourself—"

He interrupted angrily. "Lemme be. I give you what you was after, didn't I? Now leave me be."

"Sure. See you. And the hell with you." I was sorry as soon as I said it, but Joe was a nice enough guy when he was sober. He'd made me laugh plenty of times, and there are too few things to laugh at. I didn't like seeing him slopped up most of the time, so I barked at him.

He laid a hand on my arm, shaking his head. "Don't get a heat on, Scott. Just lemme be."

"Sure, Joe. Cheers." I left. The sun was almost blinding after the gloom in Manny's and I stood outside for a moment wondering if Joe had told me anything at all. The story was just crazy enough, though, that it was probably true—as true as Joe could get it. I got in the Cad and drove toward Hollywood and Polly's. A diamond bracelet with a snake's head and rubies for eyes, a guy ten feet tall, and a gal with a walk like a circus. I knew, from Joe's description, where to look for the gal: the left half of a duplex. It was worth a check.

4.
S HE WAS a tall, willowy tomato with dark hair and the unashamed curves of a modern Venus in white sweater, black skirt and spike-heeled pumps, and she came out of the duplex on Wilcox Street like a gal in a hurry. I hadn't got a good look at her since I'd staked out near the duplex on the corner, but in the hour I'd waited for her to show I'd deduced a few interesting things about her from the frilly black underthings hanging on a line behind her place. But not even the transparent and abbreviated step-ins hanging there, nor Joe's fuzzy words, had prepared me for her walk. Walk?

That wasn't a walk; it was a parade. Wilcox Street should have been curved into a horseshoe lined with bald-headed pappies chipping their choppers and falling down in dead faints while a band played "Put The Blame On Mame, Boy!" And there should have been a drum. I fell in about fifteen yards behind her and followed, let's face it, grimly intent on my job and wondering how she made any forward progress at all.

After two blocks she still hadn't looked back. I was carrying a brown tweed coat over one arm and a hat in my hand, and there were dark glasses in my shirt pocket. In case she got a look at me I could put the stuff on and look a bit different except that I'd still be six-two. But my preparations for a cagey tail seemed wasted, because she apparently didn't expect anyone to be following her. Maybe there was no reason she should have. She certainly wasn't sneaking up the street.

She kept going like that for another block and I followed her happily. Just across the next street was a small cocktail lounge with a sign over the door: Zephyr Room. She went inside. I followed her in, stopped inside the door and looked around as my eyes got accustomed to the dimness. She'd disappeared somewhere, but there were booths on the left, four or five people in them, and a bar extending from the back halfway along the right wall. This side of the bar, at its end, was a small U-shaped table with a stool behind it. I felt a little tingle of exhilaration, that must be the "kind of funny little booth thing" that Joe had mentioned. He'd been in here, all right.

I went to the bar and climbed onto a stool next to a

cowboy leaning against the bar. At least he thought he was a cowboy; he was wearing high-heeled boots and tight blue jeans, a white-trimmed black shirt, and a black neckerchief looped around his neck and tucked through a small silver cow's skull at his throat. He was real quaint.

I ordered a bourbon and water and while the bartender mixed it I reached into my inside coat pocket and took out the neatly typed list of stolen items I'd got from Osborne's jeweler. I made a few random check-marks on it with a pencil, not being careful about hiding the list from possibly prying eyes, and when the bartender brought my drink I turned the paper face down on the bar and asked him, "Did a sharp brunette just wobble in here?"

"Wobble?" He looked puzzled, then he grinned. "You must mean Lois. Yeah, she'll be out in a minute." He jerked his head toward the U-shaped table. "Dice girl."

"Thanks." I started to pull at my highball when the cowboy flipped me on the shoulder with his fingers.

"What makes you so curious?" he said. His voice was soft and gritty, like sand running through an hour glass. I didn't say anything and he said, "Well?" and flipped me again with his fingers.

I wasn't even looking at the guy, minding my drink and my business, but just that fast I was mad enough to hit him with the bar. Maybe I'm touchy, maybe I'm even a little neurotic about it, but this guy had done the wrong things—a couple of them. In the first place, I don't mind strangers blabbing at me or asking questions—if they ask them nice; he wasn't asking nice. And in the second place I don't like guys flipping me or grabbing me or even laying their paws on me.

I swallowed at my drink, then wheeled on my stool and looked at the foolish character just as he said, "I asked you a question, pally."

I took a good look at him this time. He was about an inch under six feet and broad, big-chested, and with more hair sticking up from his shirt than I've got on my head. His face was square, and his eyes were narrowed, lips pressed together as he looked at me.

I said, "I heard you. Don't ask me questions, don't call me pally, and keep your hands off me." I turned back to the bar and got the highball glass just to my lips when he latched onto my arm and pulled me around.

He started to say something, but I slammed my glass down on the bar and climbed off my stool as liquor squirted up and spread over the mahogany. I grabbed the guy by his scarf and said, "Listen, pardner, the next time you lay a hand on me you better take off those high heels and get your feet planted square on the floor, because I'll knock you clear into the men's room."

His mouth dropped open and for a moment he sputtered in surprise, then his chin snapped up and his face got white. He wrapped a hand around my wrist and drew back his right fist so he could slug me, and I almost felt sorry for what was going to happen to the cowboy. Even if he couldn't know I was an ex-Marine crammed full of more judo and unarmed defense than I knew what to do with, he should never have tried hauling off while I still had hold of his pretty scarf and he was wide open from all directions.

But he was stupid, and he actually launched his right fist at me. I gave just a little tug on the scarf and he staggered maybe two inches and the fist missed me by four inches, and he was so far off balance I had all the time in the world to grab his left arm above the elbow, then break his weakened hold on my wrist and force his wrist and arm behind him with my right hand. While he was still bending over and turning I locked his arm behind him, got some leverage from my hand on his shoulder, and he started to make noises. I was still trying to decide if I should break the arm for him, when the bartender swung a two-foot club against the bar top and yelled, "None of that! Shove it, boys, break it up."

He was pretty fast, because we'd been mixing it up for only a couple seconds—and I think he saved the cowboy's arm. I cooled off a little, nodded at the bartender, and pushed the cowboy ahead of me while I walked him four stools away. Then I let go of him.

"Maybe you better sit here, cowboy. You must have thought I was kidding. I wasn't." I went back and got his drink and sat it in front of him. He didn't do anything more dangerous than glare at me, so I went back to my drink.

The bartender was squinting at me. I said, "Sorry," then finished the bourbon and ordered another. He made it silently and I noticed there hadn't been a peep out of any of the other half-dozen or so customers. Two of them left, but others ordered more drinks. A little conversation started up again.

I asked the bartender, "Where is the men's room, anyway?" He pointed toward a door in the rear wall and I got up, leaving the list on the bar, and went back to the john. I went in, slammed the door, then cracked it and peeked through. The cowboy rubbed his arm, glanced at the paper on the bar then looked back toward the rest room. He was curious about me. Five more seconds and he got up, walked to my stool and said something to the bartender, then turned the paper over and studied it for half a minute before he slammed it back down on the bar and walked toward me and then out of my sight.

I went back to my stool. The bartender had mopped up my spilled drink and I said, "Freshen that up, will you? You got a phone booth in here?"

He nodded and pointed toward the back of the bar and around to the right. That was where my cowboy had gone. I tucked the list back into my pocket, had a swallow of my drink. In another minute the cowboy came back. He walked up beside me and smiled stiffly.

"Say," he said. "I wanna apologize. About gettin' hot."

I grinned at him. "Sure. Maybe we're both a little touchy."

He looked damned uncomfortable, but he stuck out his hand. "No hard feelings?"

"Okay by me." I shook his hand.

He lowered his voice a little and said, "I didn't mean to sound nosy, but the thing is, a good friend of mine is real innerested in Lois, see? So naturally I'm curious. You, uh, know Lois?"

I shook my head.

"You just think she's cute, huh?"

"That's right. I just think she's cute."

"Yeah," he said. "Uh, I'd feel bad if you didn't lemme buy you a drink. No hard feelings, you know; lemme buy you a drink."

I hesitated and he said to the bartender, "Hey, Frank, give my friend anything he wants, see? Gimme the same."

Right then I caught movement at the corner of my eye and turned to see Lois walking toward us from the rear of the club. Evidently there was a room back there where she'd changed because she now had on an ankle-length green gown. She walked past us and said to the bartender, "A cool one like this, Frank." She nodded at the cowboy, and then her eyes brushed briefly over mine. I grinned at her as she went by, and after a couple more steps she looked back over her shoulder, and she must have seen where I was looking, then she was at the dice table and reached up to turn on a bright light above it. I'd had a good gander at her as she walked past us, and the view was even better with her under that bright light.

The green dress came clear up to her throat then swept down over her body, clinging to her skin like a thin rubber dress a size too small. I'd have given eight to five that she wasn't wearing a thing under that dress, not a thing, not even frilly things. The dress was like green skin and I decided I could even get used to green skin if it were on Lois.

The bartender mixed up a drink, also green, and sat it on the end of the bar, then gave the cowboy and me our highballs. I picked mine up, got the green thing from the end of the bar, and walked to the dice table.

I handed her the drink. "This must be yours."

She smiled. "Uh-huh. To match my dress. Pink Ladies for a red dress, creme de cacao for brown. This is creme de menthe."

I pressed my luck. "I thought for a minute the dress was made out of creme de menthe."

She didn't mind. She smiled and said, "You like it?"

"It's terrific. Clever idea, too. What do you wear with champagne?"

She laughed, and the laugh itself was a little bit like champagne, a soft, bubbling sound that came from far down in her white throat. "That's a rhetorical question, isn't it?"

"Frankly, no." The overhead light burned soft red spots in her dark hair, hair that hung just above shoulder length. It wasn't quite black, as I'd thought at first, but an off shade like the bar mahogany, a shadow darkness with touches of deep red in it. I had known a couple of dice girls in Hollywood and several in San Francisco, where they're more often seen. Some of them were near idiots, and some were brilliant women who could have been high-powered women executives but made so much at the tables that they stuck to the game. One thing, though, all of them had in common: they were beautiful women, the kind men would look at, women who could make men cheerfully lose a dime or a thousand bucks. Lois was no exception, and she didn't sound or look stupid. Her face was oval, with dark brown eyes and warm-looking red lips, lips that were still smiling now with white, even teeth behind them.

I reached for my wallet and started to take a buck out of it, then changed my mind and found a twenty, laid it on the green felt.

"What part of that?" she asked.

"All of it. I feel lucky."

"I like to tell the nice fellows they can't win in the long run."

"Thanks," I said. I looked at her, at the way the dice table fit just over her thighs as she sat on the low stool, light pouring down over her shoulders and silvering the tops of her breasts, highlighting their thrusting tips and leaving pools of shadow beneath them, and I added, "But they can't lose."

She looked at me for long seconds, her brown eyes half-lidded; then she said, "Shoot it all."

She shoved one of the leather shakers over to me and I rattled the dice and then rolled them up against the board. She looked at them, called my points and picked up the other shaker, held it in front of her and shook the dice vigorously.

She rolled the dice. "See?" she said. "You lose."

I grinned. "That breaks me. What am I going to do for dinner tonight?"

"I don't know," she smiled. "Will you really go hungry?"

"Maybe I can bum a meal."

"Maybe. Are you really broke?"

"Uh-huh. Just fishing. Carefully."

"You don't look like the careful type."

"Depends."

I had noticed something block out the dim light coming in through the entrance. I'd been so interested in conversation that I hadn't looked around, but now the cowboy stepped up on my left.

"Hey, pally," he said.

I very clearly heard him say "pally." I looked at him. There was a tight grin on his square face. "Remember a friend of mine was innerested in Lois?"

"So he's innerested. So am I. So what?"

"So here's my good friend, pally," He jerked a thumb. I looked around at where I figured the guy's face would be and I was looking, so help me, at his tie clasp. I looked up. And up. And there it was. He wasn't a man, but a monstrosity. When I found his face I didn't recognize the features right away because I'd been too busy wondering when I'd get to it, but a few seconds after I saw the long thin head with the bony cheekbones and long sharp nose, the wide-spaced dark eyes and high forehead dwindling into wispy brown hair, I made him. Once you've seen a guy that big, you don't have much trouble remembering him.

5. BACK in '45 you couldn't pick up a sports page without seeing his name and face. He'd been in college then, *the* basketball star of the States, center on the Indians, national high-scorer. Too big for any of the services, he'd made a name for himself on the courts. Maybe you remember his name. Tommy Matson, and they called him Cannonball Matson. Since then the nickname had been shortened to Cannon. In '46 he'd turned pro, finally been kicked out of the game because of excessive roughness, near brutality—and because he'd been questioned by the San Francisco D.A. about some fixed games; questioned and let go.

After that he'd drifted. His name didn't hit the sports pages any more, but I remembered he'd been picked up for battery, released, then did a bit for second-degree burglary, a daylight job on which he hadn't carried a gun. The last I heard he'd been arrested in San Francisco, this time for first-degree burglary, a night job, but again he'd been without a gun. Cannon had been sent to San Quentin for that one. I'd brushed against him a few times on cases of mine, but I'd never been on his tail. He knew me, though, and didn't like me; I'd helped put a couple of his friends away.

I could feel my throat tighten up. The guy wasn't ten feet tall, he was a long six-feet-nine and a lumpy three hundred pounds, but Joe's story wasn't so crazy any more.

This was the boy Joe had seen in here yesterday. I turned around with my back to the dice table and said, "Hello, Cannon. I heard you fell from 'Frisco. Didn't know you were down this way."

"Now you know." He looked past me to Lois. "This chump bothering you, honey?"

"He's not bothering me, Cannon."

"I figure he is."

I butted in. "I think the lady knows more about it than you do, Cannon. And you know my name. It's not chump."

The cowboy said, "It's pally. Ain't that right, pally?"

I looked at him. "You got a short memory, friend. Next time I'll put a hinge in your elbow." Actually, right at that moment, I didn't feel too happy about all this. Another guy had come inside with Cannon and was standing by him. He was a little short guy about six feet tall, slim, bald, about forty-five. There was a scar, probably a knife scar, on his forehead just where his hairline should have been. That made four guys lined up against me, counting Cannon as two.

"Move along, Scott," Cannon said.

"I'm busy." I turned my back on him and said to Lois, "Guess we were interrupted. And I was just about to ask you something."

She was frowning, biting her lower lip. "I know," she said.

From behind me Cannon said softly, "I want you should blow, Scott, and keep going, and don't come back."

I felt a hand yank on my arm. As it spun me around I saw that it was the cowboy pulling at me and I made a mistake and concentrated on him. He got hold of my coat sleeves with both hands just as I started to chop at his face with the edge of my palm and maybe cave his face in for him, but I was concentrating on the wrong guy.

I heard Cannon grunt on my left, and I saw the big fist swooping down at my head, and I rolled with the punch just a fraction of a second too late. I was rolling when he hit me, and I damn near rolled over the dice table into Lois' lap, and a gray film dropped down over my eyes. My muscles were suddenly like jelly, and when I felt Cannon's big hand bunch up my coat and pull me toward him I was having a hard enough time keeping my legs straight under me, much less getting a fist up to his chin. I fought to clear my head as I heard Cannon say huskily, "I said blow, and stay the hell gone," and then I saw the dim blur of his fist looming up in front of me again, and just as I rolled my head to the side my head finally cleared. Everything got very clear and very black.

6.   I was in a booth. It seemed pretty sure that I was in a booth, but I didn't yet know where the booth was. I had just got my face up off the table and slowly I remembered what had happened. I wiggled my jaw, and pain cleared fog from my brain. I looked around. Lois was walking from the bar toward me, and because my eyes hadn't yet focused properly it was as though there were two of Lois walking at me, and the way just one of her navigated this was almost more than man could bear. But when she reached the table she was back to one, and it was a one-shot glass she put in front of me.

"Brandy," she said.

"Thanks." I drank it, waited half a minute, then started to stand up. "Where is that—that—that—"

I was coming out of the booth when she put a hand on my chest and said, "Sit down. I admire your stupidity, but they've left. Hadn't you better relax for a while?"

"I've been relaxed for a long while." I sat down and as she slid into the seat opposite me I said, "What's going on out there now?"

"Nothing. All the customers left too."

"They show remarkable good sense."

"Cannon and Tinkle and Artie looked through your clothes and wallet, then put everything back and left."

"That's great." I thought for a minute. "Tinkle?" I asked her. "Tinkle Miller?" It had to be; there wouldn't be another hoodlum with the same monicker.

"Uh-huh, the cowboy. And Artie Payne. And you're Shell Scott. A detective."

I looked across the table at her. "True. Is that bad?"

"I didn't say that. But it made me—wonder."

"Yeah. I suppose it would." I didn't add anything to that; I wasn't going to con the gal; she could take her chances or leave them. I said, "I didn't know you'd chosen Cannon."

"I didn't. He chose me. He's—after me, you might say. But he hasn't got me yet."

"I imagine he'd put on quite a campaign. He'd have to. You know, flowers, candy, pretty baubles, things like that."

"Things like that. He ordered me to stay away from you."

"I had you picked as a gal to ask, not to order."

"I am."

"Well, I'm asking."

"What and when?"

"Dinner. Tonight."

"Maybe." She glanced toward the door. "Couple customers," she said. "I have to get back to the table." She left. Naturally I watched her walk away.

I ordered and slowly drank a last water-high while I added some bits and pieces. Tinkle Miller. A hood who'd been lucky with convictions, but had been charged with half the book, mostly suspicion of burglary. A Jack-of-all-trades hoodlum, he'd been a dishwasher, bank clerk and burglar, labor goon and locksmith, soda jerk and short-con man, strikebreaker, and, of course, a cowboy. I filed the one important point in my aching head and added some more. Yesterday Joe had stumbled in here in an alcoholic haze, seen Cannon bestowing a pretty bauble on Lois. I wondered about Lois. Today Tinkle Miller had seen a similar pretty bauble among those on my typed list, called Cannon and Artie Payne, and Cannon had proceeded to knock me silly. It looked pretty good. I got up.

On my way out I stopped at the dice table. Lois was alone there and I said, "Well?"

She nibbled on the inside of her lip. "Where we going?"

"Grove okay?"

"Cocoanut Grove?"

"Uh-huh. Then the Strip, Ciro's, Mocambo, maybe catch Kay Thompson and the Williams Brothers."

"Your face is already swollen. Won't you mind?"

"I'll put ice packs on it."

"I'm supposed to work."

"Get a headache. Then we'll be even."

"All right."

"You got a long slinky dress you feel like trying out?"
She smiled. "Umm-hmmm. Long—and low."

"Wonderful." I grinned at her. "What color?"

She looked up at the ceiling, then slanted her eyes
down at me, lips curving into an amused smile, slightly
wicked. "Rum and coke."

"The time and the place?"

She scribbled on a paper and handed it to me. I looked
at it and said, "So long, Lois. See you at nine."

"So long, Shell. Don't be late."

"You kidding?" I left. It was just getting dark. . . .

I reached the Spartan Apartment Hotel, home, at seven
P.M. Inside I mixed a weak drink, then settled on the over-
sized chocolate brown divan in the front room, winked at
Amelia, the nude over my fake fireplace, and put in a call
to Diane Borden.

"Hello-o?"

"Diane? Shell Scott. I want—"

"Ooooh, Scotty. How nice. You missed me. Really
missed me."

"No. I want—"

"You didn't miss me? Scotty! Please!"

"Okay, I missed you. Now listen. Reserve two tables at
the Ambassador tonight. The Grove, adjoining tables. If
you need glasses, wear them—"

"I don't need glasses—"

"Keep quiet a minute. One table is for you; the other
is for me and a gal. I'm hoping she'll be wearing some
rocks. Maybe yes, maybe no, but just in case, I want you
to be there to take a peek. If you see anything that looks
like yours, just sit tight. I'll get the word from you; I'll
table-hop or something. Okay?"

"What are you talking about?"

I went through it again, more slowly and clearly, telling
her to get the tables for nine-thirty, and she said, "Is she
pretty?"

"Who?"

"The girl."

"Yeah, she's a beauty. What's that got to do with your
bracelet and chokers and—" I broke it off. "Oh, hell, I
forgot. Drink cokes or something till we get there."

"I'll drink anything I want."

"But you'll get in—"

"You dope. I'm twenty-one. I told you I was—"

"You're what!"

"Twenty-one. You can look it up if you want to, just like a detective. I was twenty-one six days ago. So there."

She hung up.

Well, I thought. Well, well. . . .

It was nine sharp when I read the neat card, "Lois Sanders," and rang the buzzer. A gong went off inside, then she opened the door and a gong went off in my head. This time she was in a gown like deep maroon skin, just the right size. The dress wasn't high on her throat like the green one; it was strapless, smooth, low on her high breasts, snug around her trim waist, gleaming over her curving hips, gracefully draped almost to the floor.

"Come in," she said. "You're right on time. And you know something? My headache is miraculously gone."

I stared at her. "You know something? *I* am miraculously gone. You look lovely, Lois." She held the door and I went inside.

"Thank you," she said. "You're rather pretty, too. You look right at home in a dinner jacket."

I'd showered and shaved and climbed into the old tux and black tie. If I'd had soup and fish I'd probably have worn the silly things. I wanted this to be "formal" enough so Lois would feel lost without some glittering jewelry. Funny thing, though, I was beginning to feel a little lousy about this deal.

Lois took both my hands in hers and backed across the room to a divan that faced a wide window.

"You sit there, Shell. Drink before we leave?"

"Swell."

"You'll have to take what I've got. But it's not too bad."

She was still holding my hands, her back to the window and faint illumination behind her softly outlining the curve of her waist and hips. "Sounds delightful," I said, and tightened my hands on hers.

She slipped her fingers free and said, smiling, "I meant rum and coke."

"I was afraid you meant something like that."

I looked out the window until she came back with the drinks. We chatted about nothing in particular, pleasantly, so pleasantly that I didn't want it to end and decided I liked Lois perhaps a bit too well. It was nine-fifteen when we finished our drinks.

"Ready, Lois?"

"Uh-huh. I'll get my stole."

I followed her to the bedroom door. She picked what looked like a mink stole off the bed, draped it over her shoulders and walked back in front of me. She didn't have on a single diamond, ruby, bracelet or necklace. She wasn't even wearing a ring.

I opened my mouth to comment on that, and stopped. This wasn't at all clever or funny any more. But finally I said, "Here I am all decked out in studs and links and a he-mannish after-shave lotion, and you haven't so much as a watch. I'll have to buy you some baubles."

It came out flat, toneless, and cruelly obvious. I had no way of knowing what Cannon might have said to her earlier in the Zephyr Room. Nor what he'd said yesterday when he gave her what I felt sure was Diane's bracelet. She could know Cannon had given her a stolen bracelet, she might even be in with him; she might suspect the thing was stolen, or she might think it was a paste offering from a smitten suitor. And she might not even have it now, whether it was the one I was after or another one entirely—but I had to find out, and I was stuck now with the way I'd played it.

If Lois had wondered, during the evening or earlier, if I'd say anything about her wearing jewelry, she hadn't given any indication of it. She'd been sweet and happy and smiling, but now the half-smile went away from her face and something went out of her brown eyes.

"Maybe you're right, Shell," she said. "I suppose I should wear something."

She turned away from me and went to a dresser against the left wall, opened the second drawer and took out a square box. "Well, help me out," she said, not looking at me. "What should I wear?"

She opened the box and watched me as I walked over and looked down into it at the crystal-white stones, and the red ones, the bracelets and chains and pins.

And it was there. The bracelet with the snake's head, ruby-red eyes, and a forked gold tongue flicking out of the mouth. I picked it up.

"How about this?"

Right then, if it was all going to come apart, was when it should have happened. But she went along with it, neither of us fooling the other. "All right," she said quietly.

I picked up a glistening choker, gems set into a thin black band. "This would be good."

"It's rhinestones. I bought it myself. Most of the others were given to me." She swallowed. "By men, of course."

I lifted her wrist. She'd already slipped the bracelet on and I asked, "More rhinestones?"

"I don't know. I don't think so." She hesitated. "Cannon gave it to me, Shell. I suppose you know that."

"I . . . I had a hunch, honey."

She was facing me, and she put the choker around her throat, her hands behind her neck to fasten it there. Her full breasts lifted and pressed against the edge of her dress. She said softly, "I don't know why I'm putting this on. I hope you didn't make reservations."

I winced. "Look, Lois. Let's get this straight. We might as well now. Cannon gave you the rocks. I think they're hot—stolen. There you've got it. I didn't know I was going to get into a screwed-up mess like this, but there it is. Now what about it? Anything you can tell me? Or should I keep on guessing?"

Her brown eyes were icy. "Cannon gave me this yesterday. I don't know where he got it or how—and up till now I didn't want to know. He's given me other things, but never anything so nice. He's been trying to—buy something from me, by giving me things, but he hasn't bought anything yet because it's not for sale. Or maybe he has bought something." She paused, looking at me, her oval face sober, then added, "And I don't like you at all, Shell."

Neither of us said anything after that for a while, but finally I said, "I wonder whatever made me think I was a detective? Hey, what say we have another quick one, then take off for the high spots."

"You still want to go?" Her voice was dull.

"Sure."

We each had a short drink and some rather deadly and dragging conversation, and then we left. She was awfully quiet going down in the elevator and I said, "Lois, honey, give me a grin. Let out a whoop or something. Come on, we'll have a big kick tonight, let down your hair."

She smiled slightly. "I suppose there's no sense wasting the evening."

"Of course not. We'll run around screeching, we'll get higher than rockets and yip at people. Baby, we'll dance in the streets—" The elevator stopped, so I stopped, but she shook her head at me and the smile was a little wider, a little brighter.

She looped her arm through mine and we went out onto Wilcox Street. I steered her toward the Cad, but just before we reached it I heard something scrape on the sidewalk and Lois said, "Why Cannon! What—"

And then there was a grunt, and a great whistling and roaring and clanging of bells, and my last sad thought after that monstrous fist landed like an artillery shell alongside my head was: There'll be no dancing in the streets tonight.

7. I CAME to this time in my Cad, slumped behind the wheel. The first time this had happened, I had been more than a bit peeved at Cannon. But now I was seriously considering killing the son. I was so mad that it felt as if the top of my head were going to pop off and sail through the roof of the Cad like a flying saucer. It was five minutes before I calmed down enough to start thinking about anything except smashing my fists into Cannon's ugly face.

Then I got out of the car and went back to Lois's apartment. She wasn't there; at least there was no response to my ringing the buzzer and banging on the door. I checked the Zephyr Room but Lois had "gone home with a headache" and hadn't come back. No, neither Cannon nor his pals had been in. Yes, I did have a black eye, and would you like a couple? I left the Zephyr Room and went back to my apartment, still burning.

It was a little after ten. I looked up Lois Sanders in the phone book and called her half a dozen times, but each time the line was busy. Finally I flopped on the bed, still in my tux. The phone ringing woke me at midnight.

I woke up with everything still fresh in my mind, grabbed the phone and I suppose I snarled into it, "Yeah?"

"Scotty . . . Scotty, I'm plastered. Oh, woo, am I drunk. Scotty? That you, Scotty?"

I groaned. Diane. Oh, Lord, now Diane. I'd completely

forgotten about her. I said, "Where the hell are you?"

"I'm at the Groove, Coc'nut Groove, an' you're not here, Scotty, you're not here."

She sounded moist. I said roughly, "For Pete's sake don't bust out bawling. I'll come down and get you."

"Will you? Will you, Scotty?"

"Yes, of course. Just hang on, I'll be there in fifteen or twenty minutes."

She said, "Goodie," and I hung up. Well, at least I was dressed for the Grove. Almost. I hadn't been wearing my gun up till now. I went into the bedroom, dug out the .38 Colt Special and shrugged out of my jacket, slipped on the gun and harness. With the jacket back on it bulged over the gun, but that was all right. Now I was dressed. If I saw Cannon, and he so much as sneered at me, I was going to aim at his right eye and pull the trigger. Then when he fell down I was going to aim at his left eye and pull the trigger. Then I was going to kick him in the head, real hard.

In the bathroom I took a look at myself, and I looked terrible. The left side of my jaw was swollen considerably and my right eye was purple and almost closed. I could see out of it still; well enough to aim a .38 anyway. I headed back toward the front room and somebody outside pressed the buzzer. I opened the door and gawked at the guy in a gray suit and the cop in uniform.

"What's the matter?" I asked them. I know a lot of guys in the department, but these were strangers.

"You're Scott?"

"Yeah."

"Better come with us."

"Huh? What for? What is this?"

They were both medium height, both husky, one about twenty-five, the other in his forties. The older one was in plain clothes, the other in a patrolman's uniform.

The older guy showed me his shield and said, "Where'd you leave your Cad, Scott?"

"It's down in front. I parked it on the street, sure, so I get a ticket. I was pooped, and—"

He interrupted. "What happened to your face? You have an accident?"

"I was in a fight. I guess it was a fight. This some new kind of traffic citation?"

"No ticket, Scott. Hit and run. You didn't leave your car on the street. Not this street."

"What?" It hadn't even penetrated.

He smelled my breath. "Drunk? All sharped up, too. You usually have fights in those clothes?" His voice hardened. "Come on with us, Scott. We want you to look at somebody. In the morgue."

We were in the prowl car and headed toward downtown L.A. before it hit me. Oh, my God, I thought. Not . . . not Lois.

They took me downstairs in the Hall of Justice and back into the morgue. The body was covered with the usual cloth and they stood me alongside the table and peeled the cloth back.

The plainclothesman said, "Well? You know who it is?"

I felt sick. I said, "I've told you twenty times you've got the wrong guy. I didn't do it." I looked at the battered corpse again. "But I know who it is. His name was Joseph Raspberry."

The next few hours were long ones, and lousy ones. It seemed that I answered a thousand questions a thousand times each, but finally the pressure eased off a little. About twenty of the cops I know in the department, all friends of mine, came around and they were on my side as much as they could be. Even Phil Samson, Captain of Homicide and my best friend in L.A., climbed out of bed and roared down when word reached him. He threw his substantial weight about the place for half an hour; and I about half convinced the cops that I wouldn't slam into a guy with my car, then leave the car out where it could be spotted.

The police story was simple enough, once I got it. Calls concerning both the body lying at the side of a darkened road and the black Cadillac coupe convertible parked a mile away had come in at almost the same time, close to eleven-thirty P.M. The Cad's right front fender was caved in, with blood and bits of hair on it. My name, of course, was on the Cad's registration slip. The cops had looked into the trunk, too, where I keep all kinds of gadgets useful in my work, ranging from loaded grenades to an infra-red optophone, and not knowing me they'd figured I was either a master criminal or a mad scientist about to blow up the city. But that was all squared away when Samson and some of the other cops came around at headquarters.

My story was simple enough, too: I told them exactly what I'd done all evening, except that I didn't mention the fact that Joe had given me the tip that set me off—I had a season—and I didn't mention Cannon's name. I just told them I didn't see who had slugged me and I figured it was a jealous suitor, which was true. My car obviously had been stolen and used to rub out Joe, apparently, I said, by somebody who wanted to give me trouble, and had.

It was long and wearisome, and the only break was when, at one-thirty in the morning, I sprang out of my chair and almost to the ceiling yelling "Jesus, Diane!" It had come to me in a flash that she was probably lying under the table by now, her eyes glassy. Samson was ready to leave then, so he said he'd pick her up and see that she got home and—ha, ha—tell her I was in jail.

The upshot of it all was that I got mugged and printed, but out on bail shortly after eight A.M. Before nine I was back in my office without the thousand-dollar bill in my kick, all the morning papers spread on the desk before me, and the gripe, the anger, the fury in me feeding on itself and growing big enough to fill all Los Angeles and a substantial part of the universe.

I had a good deal of information now, facts which satisfied me but wouldn't last two seconds in court, even though one fact led to another and another right up to the valid conclusion. Naturally the boy I wanted was Cannon. But I had to tie him up so tight he'd never wriggle out. And I had to do it my way, do it myself, and do it fast. And for several reasons.

If I didn't, I was probably through as a private investigator, at least in L.A. I've mentioned that a detective wouldn't last six months without his informants and stools. The guys in and around the rackets would know by now that Joe had tipped me, and that Joe had been given the canary treatment. I knew that right now in the underworld of Los Angeles the word was spreading, the rumble was going from bar to back room to poker game to horse parlor: "They got Scott's canary." And the unspoken question would be, what was I going to do about it.

One of the things demanded of the guy tipped is that he protect or cover for the tipster; canaries stop singing when it isn't profitable. If I sat still, most of my tips and leaks would slow and eventually stop. I could have told the cops what I thought and let them pick up Cannon and his chums, question them, and with nothing solid against them let them go—whereupon Cannon would sit back and laugh at me, and so would the rest of the hoods and hooligans. No, I had to get him myself, and get him good.

There was more reason, too. I looked at the newspapers on my desk. Only one of them had the story headlined, but all of them had something about it on the front page. The stories merely said I was being questioned—I'd still been in the can when the reporters got the word—but they all had my name spelled correctly. Too many people would automatically figure me for the hit and run, even though my friends would know better. Most newspaper readers never see the "alleged" and "authoritative source" and "suspicion of." They take the conjectures as facts and you're hung on the newspaper's banner. I was. A year from now a lot of people hearing the name Shell Scott would say, "Yeah, he run over that little guy."

My office phone rang and I grabbed it, feeling like biting off the mouthpiece. It was Jules Osborne.

"Mr. Scott? What's happened? Have you seen the papers? Diane phoned me last night. She was drunk; it was terrible. And I don't know what—this is—"

"Don't get giddy. And yeah, I've seen the papers. What the hell do you want?"

"Why, I . . ." he sputtered a little. "Naturally I was concerned. I . . ."

"Look, Mr. Osborne. I've had a trying night. I know what I'm doing, and I'm getting close to what you want. Just relax for a while and read the papers."

I listened to him chatter for a bit, then I said, "No, I didn't mention you to the cops—I won't. Nobody knows a thing. And I won't put a word on paper, no reports or anything."

"But Diane—she's all upset. What—"

"I'll talk to Diane. I'll chew her ear off. She won't bother you. Good-by." I hung up. I just didn't feel easy going.

And I was pooped. I'd had only about an hour and a half of sleep—not including the two short periods at the Zephyr Room and behind the wheel of my Cad, which didn't count. My jaw hurt, my right eye was damn near closed, and I was wandering around in broad daylight in that stupid tuxedo. My Cad was being gone over by the lab boys and I wouldn't get it back till this afternoon, so I left the office, flagged a cab, and told the driver to take me out to Hollywood and the Spartan Apartment Hotel.

Diane's house wasn't out of the way, so I had the driver wait while I went to her door and rang. It took her so long to get to the door and open it that I'd almost decided she wasn't home. But finally dragging feet came unsteadily through the front room, the door opened, and a strand of red hair and one blood-shot blue eye peered out at me. There were no glad cries this morning.

"Oh," she said. "You."

"Me. I dropped by to tell you I'm sorry about last night."

"*You're* sorry!"

"Samson pick you up?"

"That old man?"

"He's not so old."

"That's what you think."

What I thought was that Samson, a happily married man who never looked at another woman unless she was about to be booked, must have had one hell of a time with this little tomato. But I said, "And I wanted to ask you to lay off Osborne. Every time you yak at him he yaks at me and I've got no time for yakking. I'll get your pretties back."

"Oh, foo," she said, then told me without humor what I could do with her pretties. She wasn't very gay this morning, either. I left.

After a shower and change to a gabardine suit, complete with gun and holster, I phoned Lois at her apartment. No answer. I went back into downtown L.A., into the back rooms again, the smelly bars, and the horse parlors. I hit hotels and rooming houses, and I spent six hours and four hundred dollars, and sometimes I was a little brutal, but I was in a hurry. I got what I was after. Like the dope from Slip Kelly, for one thing.

I found Slip shooting pool in a dump on the wrong

side of Main Street. I took him back into the men's room, shut the door and leaned against it.

"Slip, I guess you heard about Joe."

"Joe Raspberry?"

"Come off it. You know what Joe."

He licked his lips. "Yeah. It—was in the papers."

"Sure. So now you tell me every goddam thing you know about Cannon and Tinkle and Artie Payne."

"Huh? I don't know nothin'—"

I didn't lay a hand on him, but I said, "Shut up. I know you do. You practically grew up with Tinkle and you did a bit at Quentin with Artie. Listen steady, Slip. Big Foster's back in town. He knows I puked on him at the trial, but he doesn't know who belched to me. He'd sure like to know."

It didn't take him long to figure that one out. He frowned and said, "You couldn't do nothin' like that."

"I could, Slip. And I would. The squeeze is on. I'm in a spot, man. I'm a little mad about Joe, too. And nobody would ever know I finked on you except you and me. And Foster. And then just me and Foster."

He told me what I wanted to know.

Dazzy Brown was a knocked-out, easygoing colored boy who played trumpet so sweet it made Harry James sound like a man with a kazoo, and Dazzy inhaled marijuana smoke as if it were oxygen. He'd been in stir for stealing eight saxophones and a trombone, so he knew what stir was like, and I sidled up to him at a west-side bar, threw a friendly arm around his shoulders, planted my chops three inches from his and said softly, "Listen, cat, I just learned you grow that gage in flower pots, so come along with me, boy, you're going to the house of many slammers where they don't play no blues," and it was remarkable the way he cooperated.

Then there was Hooko Carter, the long-nosed grifter with a heroin habit, who had never given me the time of day before this, but who was going to give me all twenty-four hours very soon now. I got him out of bed in his rooming house, and he didn't have anything to say either. At first. So I told him:

"Hooko, you're my pal, I want you to know that. You're also Artie Payne's pal; and there's a rumble you and Cannon used to be closer than Siamese twins. Something else I know: it costs you forty skins a day for reindeer dust, and you need that steady supply. You get it from Beetle, but you don't know where he gets it. I do, but I don't have enough on the guy to put him away—just enough so he wouldn't like antagonizing me. He'd be glad to do me a favor. What's it like when you can't get your dynamite, pal?"

So I got a little more from Hooko. By four o'clock in the afternoon I'd made a few more enemies, and one gunsel had spit through his teeth at me, and maybe he'd do it again, but he sure wouldn't do it through teeth. I'd been a real rip-roaring wildcat, all right, and a lot of the things I did I wouldn't have done on an ordinary day, but this was no ordinary day—and I'd got what I wanted, even more than I'd expected.

And one thing was sure: there was a new rumble in the back rooms and bars and hangouts now, the grapevine was twitching and hoodlums and hipsters were bending ears all over town. The question now wouldn't be: What's Scott going to do about it, but Who's gonna get killed? The canaries would feel a little better, and keep on singing, but I wondered what Cannon and Tinkle and Artie would be thinking now. Because they'd be on the grapevine too; they'd know I was throwing a lot of weight around, leaning on them, even though they wouldn't know for sure what I'd learned or what I was going to do next. But Cannon would know by now that I figured on killing him.

I'd found out for damn sure what I'd already been sure of, that Cannon and Tinkle and Artie were the boys who'd been pulling the ten-to-two jobs—and most important of all I learned there was a job set up for tonight. If the job went through, there'd be four of us in on it; if it didn't, I'd try another way. From bits and pieces I'd made my plan.

From Hooko I found out, among a lot of unimportant things, that Artie Payne was called the "Professor" because he had such a valuable think-pot, and because he'd been librarian at Folsom for three years; from Slip I learned the Professor had worked in the Westinghouse labs from the time he was twenty-six till he was thirty-four, and he'd naturally learned a lot about lighting, all kinds of lighting and lights. I already knew Tinkle, the Cowboy, had been a locksmith. And I figured, from personal experience, that Cannon could break a man's neck with one blow of his big fist if he hit him squarely with his three-hundred pounds behind it. It was adding up, fitting together.

At two-thirty in the afternoon I put in a third phone call to Lois. I'd called her a second time at one, but there hadn't been any answer then either. So I hadn't seen or talked to her since that sad moment when she'd said, "Why, Cannon. What—" and I'd heard Cannon grunt as he started to swing. But I'd done a lot of wondering. I'd just about rejected any idea that she was "in" with Cannon on any of his capers—it was hardly likely she'd have showed me the hot rocks he'd handed her if she were—but whether she'd known the stones were stolen or not I didn't know. I kind of leaned toward the idea that what she'd told me last night was true: that she hadn't known and hadn't wanted to know; the implication being that the snake-eyed hoop was a damned handsome chunk of sparkles, and she hoped it was clean. And the word I'd got from the boys around town was that Lois was simply a solid tomato, on the up and up, whom Cannon was hot for. I liked it that way, because I'd begun getting somewhat steamed up about Lois myself—and I was more than a little worried about her. I thought again about how I'd felt starting for the morgue last night.

Then she answered the phone.

"Lois? Uh, Shell Scott here."

"Oh . . . hello, Shell."

"You all right?"

"Yes. How about you? I saw the papers."

"That was a frame. I'm okay; a little stooped over, but on my feet. What happened to you after I—after I left?"

Her story was that she'd gawked at Cannon while he dumped me into my Cad, then tried to slap his eyeballs out, at least so she said, then they'd had a word battle during which she'd called him all kinds of names. After a minute or two of this, they'd finally gone back into her apartment and were there when I'd banged on the door, Cannon ready to clobber her if she'd peeped—and after my departure the fireworks continued.

She went on, "It lasted about an hour, but when he left, I told him not to come back."

"I called you last night but your line was busy. What—"

"Even after Cannon left, he phoned me a couple times.

He was so persistent I took the phone off its hook and went to bed."

I was quiet for a minute, then, "Honey, I guess you haven't changed your opinion of me. Or, have you?"

"When I found out you were a detective I wondered if you wanted to take me out because you . . . let's say, just couldn't resist me, or if you had a detective's reason. So naturally I was a little disappointed last night. But then I realized you were right; I knew the kind of man Cannon was, but I took the things he gave me anyway. I feel better now, though; as long as I thought he might have bought those things for me I could enjoy them. But when I *knew* he probably stole them, naturally I gave them back."

"You what?"

"I gave them back to him. Last night."

"You what?"

"Well . . . he suggested it, and I was afraid not to. And I didn't want them any more, anyway."

I ground my teeth together. Right now I wasn't nearly as interested in the jewelry itself as I was in getting the guys who had lifted it, but I should at least have wrapped up that bracelet last night. I was even starting to wonder what could have made me so stupid as to leave the thing loose, when I remembered it was Cannon who'd made me so stupid. It was just another reason to hate him, and maybe before long it wouldn't make any difference.

I said, "Honey, listen. You shooed Cannon out last night, but do you think he'd jump at the chance to come back? If he has any sense he would."

"This might sound egotistical, but I'm sure he would. He was practically on his knees when he left. But—"

"What would you say if I asked you to get in touch with him, tell him you're sorry, that you'd like to see him tonight?"

It took her a while to answer that one, but she said, "All right, Shell. You're a very strange and thorough detective, aren't you?"

The same tone was in her voice now that had been there when I'd asked her last night to wear the bracelet. I started to explain everything, then made myself shut up. It wouldn't be any good that way. And I wondered for a moment if she could possibly be conning me. I said, "You'll do it then?"

"When am I supposed to see him and where are we going?"

"Never mind where you're going. But you want to see him around ten."

"All right. Good-by."

"Hey, I called earlier this morning but couldn't get you. What—"

"Believe it or not, I was buying some rhinestones."

She hung up. I hung up. By four-fifteen I'd finished all the checking in town I was going to do. It was quite a trio I'd been checking on: the Professor was the brain, the Cowboy was the Houdini, and the Cannon was the muscle and boss. From Hooko, who had long known Cannon well, I'd learned that he should have been called No-Cannon Cannon, because he never carried a gun; Artie and Cowboy Tinkle always kept their arms warm with heaters. I had talked to a man named Sylvester Johnson, who lived next door to the attorney who'd been killed, beaten and shot during a burglary. Sylvester's story, condensed: "Yes, sir, that night we were sitting out back by the barbecue pit, drinking beer. No, we didn't see or hear anything till Mr. Drake came home. He parked his car and went inside. About a minute after he turned on the lights we heard a shot. Called the police. No, didn't see anybody leave. Glad to help."

I'd checked the dates of all nine reported robberies— and Diane's—against weather-bureau records. They'd all been pulled off on moonless or overcast nights. All between roughly, ten and two. If people were going to be out, they'd be gone by ten; and often they were home shortly after the bars closed. A heavy fog was predicted for tonight.

It was solid enough. I called Homicide and got Samson on the phone. After the hellos I said, "Sam, I'm coming down to get my Caddy in half an hour—boys said it would be ready. You're buddies with Turner in Scientific Investigation. How about having his infra-red flashlight, and the red-lensed goggles that go with it, in the back of my Cad along with all my junk?"

"What? Why in blue hell do you want that stuff?"

"I, uh, lost something in a dark cellar. I want to go look for it. I'd be awful happy if you didn't ask me any more."

"God damn it, Shell, have you got something we need?"

"Nothing that's any good to anybody but me. And not a thing that's worth a damn as evidence—yet. That's straight, Sam. But go along with me and maybe there will be."

"I'd like to, Shell, but . . ."

"And, Sam, you saw the papers. Can't be helped, but I'd sure like some more stories in them tomorrow or the next day. A story that would rub out the smell before it sinks too far in. And besides, you don't know what I want the stuff for. Maybe I'm going out to Lover's Lane and spy on the high-school kids."

"Shell Scott shot in the head would make a nice story. And what the hell am I going to tell Turner? Well . . ." He was quiet for a few seconds. "I ought to put you in jail for sending me out to get that crazy woman last night."

"Was she trouble?"

"When I got to the Grove she was singing. Into the bloody microphone. I like to never got her out of there. And when I did—let me tell you."

I got my first good laugh of the day from his story. Then he said, "Well, hell, look in your trunk when you get down here. I can't promise anything."

"Thanks, Sam. See you."

There was no trouble getting the Cad, and Sam had left what I wanted in the trunk. The goggles looked much like red-lensed glasses, but the light was a big son of a gun, well over a foot wide, and long, perhaps four inches thick, with a curved metal handle on its top. I put them both in the front seat and drove to Eighth Street, parked before Porter's Radio Shop and went inside. This was my second trip today; I'd been here about noon. Porter, a young, studious-looking ex-G.I. came out.

"Hi, Shell. I just finished it up. That's fifty bucks."

"A hell of a price for one vacuum tube and a dry-cell battery in a beat-up cigar box."

He grinned. "You're paying, my friend, for my genius and brilliant know-how."

"I'd have made it myself if I'd had the time."

He sneered, then went into the back room and came out with the "squawk box" I'd ordered. He sat it on the counter beside the compact radio receiver complete with loop antenna. I gave Porter his fifty bucks and he frowned.

"You know, I ought to have a deposit on that receiver," he said. "Only one I got with a loop."

"I'll bring it back tomorr—" I stopped. "Maybe I'd better leave a deposit at that."

I gave him some more money, then used his phone to call Lois again. She answered right away.

"Shell, honey. Well?"

"He . . . I guess I overestimated myself. He—well, he couldn't make it. He was awfully apologetic, but he said he'd see me tomorrow instead."

I laughed. I felt like a million. "Baby," I said. "He won't see you tomorrow—or the next day, or even the next."

"Shell, I've been just sitting here for almost an hour, thinking a lot. You knew he wouldn't see me tonight, didn't you?"

"I knew he wouldn't because if he tried I was going to clobber him with a tire iron. But I did have a hunch he wouldn't try."

"Shell! Darn you, can't you let a girl in on anything?"

"I'll tell you the truth, sweetheart. I wasn't sure I could trust you."

"You sure now?"

"No. But sure enough."

"Shell, darn you—*damn* you!"

"Still friends?"

"Oh, I suppose . . ." Then her voice dropped lower, softened, got like champagne again, and I remembered her at the dice table in her creme-de-menthe gown, the way she'd looked when I'd asked her what she wore with champagne. She said, "No . . . I don't think you and I can be friends." The "friends" was slightly accented. She went on, "Shell, it seems that every time I talk to you or see you, I learn more about you."

It seemed time to try pressing my luck again. "How much would you like to learn?"

A soft chuckle was her answer. Then, "Will I see you? Later maybe?"

I thought about that. "With any luck honey, I'll see you later."

"Promise?"

"Sure, honey."

We hung up. I lugged the squawk box and receiver out

to my Cad and sat it on the front seat alongside the flash and goggles I'd got from Sam. I was ready to go.

I drove to Artie Payne's first. During the afternoon I'd learned where the Professor and the other two lived, and where Professor Payne kept his '50 Chrysler—which was used on the trio's jobs. It was dark when I reached his place, and it took me only a couple of minutes to tape the small squeal box to his car's rear axle. I brushed off my clothes and drove three miles to Cannon's hotel on National Boulevard, went four blocks past it, made a U-turn and parked, lit a cigarette and waited. The big light, red glasses, and radio receiver were on the seat beside me.

If the boys went ahead with their planned caper tonight, I knew Artie would pick up Tinkle and Cannon and they'd go from here to whatever spot they'd cased—and I couldn't think of anything else which would keep Cannon away from a repentant Lois. But they'd know what I'd been doing today, and they'd be even more jumpy than usual. A close tail was out; damn near any kind of tail was out. If they didn't find that squawk box, though, there was one tail that could work. The little cigar box on the axle of Miller's car was no more than a small and simple radio sending set which would put out a steady howl that I could pick up on the receiver beside me, locating the car's direction from me with the loop antenna.

I waited. The moon was barely past the crescent stage tonight, and it was cold. Fog had just started to drift in from the beaches a few miles away, mixing with the smog, dimming the street lights around me. I waited, smoking one cigarette after another.

I was wondering if the boys had been scared off, when I picked up a squeal while I was turning the loop antenna. It was eleven o'clock and the Professor was on his way.

8.

THE HOWL got louder in the radio receiver and I started the Cad's motor. In a minute I saw the fog-dimmed headlights of a car pull into the curb and stop four blocks away, at Cannon's hotel. Two minutes later the car started up again and took a right at the corner. Immediately the howl in my radio receiver stopped. I threw my old cigarette away and lit another.

They wouldn't take a chance on a ticket the night of

a job, so I estimated their top speed at thirty and gave them a full minute, then put the Cad in gear and swung left off National Boulevard at Sepulveda, where they'd turned. I figured they shouldn't be more than half a mile ahead of me. I pointed the loop antenna ahead, but there wasn't any squeal so I turned it around ninety degrees and kept going straight down Sepulveda, past Rose Avenue and Ocean Park Avenue and Charnock Road, and there wasn't a peep out of the radio. But at Venice Boulevard the howl came in strong and I swung left; it stayed steady so I knew they weren't going in the opposite direction. I gave the Cad more gas and closed the distance between us.

From there it was easy enough. They made only two more turns, a left at Cochran and a right at Twelfth. On Twelfth they stopped, and eight blocks after I made the last turn, I passed Artie's car, parked. Now it was going to start getting a little precarious.

I knew they wouldn't park in front of the house they'd cased, and maybe not even on the same street, but they wouldn't work too far from the car, and I at least knew where the Chrysler was. I could get them there if it came to that, but I wanted to catch them cold, right on the job. Right here was where I found out if I'd figured how they worked correctly; I didn't know for sure, but it was more than a hunch. I put on the red-lensed glasses and drove slowly ahead looking at the houses on both sides of the street. Nothing. After four blocks I went right a block then and headed back. There on Dockweiler Street, less than two blocks from where their car was parked, I passed a big two-story Georgian-type mansion dark except for a faint light showing at one upstairs window. When I took the goggles off, the house was completely dark; not a glimmer of illumination came from any part of the house. But with the glasses on again, the light was there. I'd found them.

I parked around the corner and cut the headlights and motor. Even now that I'd found them, it still seemed like magic to me. I'd worked with infra-red light before; I knew that New York Harbor boats were equipped with infra-red spotlights and binoculars, and that Army snipers picked off the enemy outlined in infra-red from scopes mounted on their rifles—but it still seemed like a trick of Merlin.

I knew my gun was ready, but I took it out of the holster and checked it again anyway, then slipped it back. My heartbeat speeded up involuntarily; my throat dried; I could feel a slight, cold shiver brush over my skin. I picked up the heavy light, shoved the goggles up on my forehead and got out of the car. Fog was damp against my face.

Near the house I slipped the glasses down over my eyes again and saw the light still visible above. I was damned careful getting to the house and walking to its front, my body pressed against the wall, but I made it without trouble to the front door. I switched the light on and in its glow I could see the door was slightly cracked. Tinkle, the ex-locksmith, wouldn't lock it again till they left; there was always a chance the boys might want to leave in a hurry. The boys were pretty positive about this job. They didn't bother to leave a lookout. I loved them for it.

Before I went through the door I slid out the .38 and held it in my right hand, the burning flash in my left. I went inside, swung the flash around till I spotted a stairway leading above, then started walking up it. I couldn't see as well as I'd have liked, but I wouldn't bump into any chairs or walls—and Cannon, Artie, and Tinkle, working in infra-red above me, wouldn't be able to see any better. For a moment I thought of the attorney these bastards had killed, wondered if he'd walked into a darkened room, unable to see a thing, while the three men above me now could watch his every movement, see to beat him, to kill him.

I followed a hall at the head of the stairs till I could see a glow from the room in which I knew they were, then I turned off my light. If I could see their light, they could also see mine. The door was ajar. I heard their soft movements, but I couldn't yet see them. I kept moving forward, slowly, my hand sweaty and slippery on the butt of my .38.

A yard from the door I pulled the Colt's hammer back on full cock and took the last step, spotted them inside the room, and then I moved through the doorway. For that first second none of them saw me. Cannon stood at the window, his back toward me; Artie was at a safe in the right wall, Tinkle holding a bulky light similar to mine, bathing Artie and the safe in infra-red light.

My heart had suddenly started racing and I could feel the blood tingling clear down in the tips of my fingers. It was as though the blood were hot inside me, warming my body. I could feel perspiration on my face and chest, in my armpits. I tightened my finger on the Colt's trigger and snapped on the beam of my flash just as Artie glanced over his shoulder, eyes behind the goggles like round black holes in a skull's head, and spotted me.

I saw his mouth open and I shouted, "Freeze, you sons, don't—" but that was all I had time for because a lot of hell broke loose in that instant. Artie yelled at the top of his lungs and leaped to the side as Tinkle spun around and the light he'd held thudded to the carpet, still burning. Cannon's huge bulk dropped to the floor. I flipped my gun over at Cannon, rolling now toward the wall, but flame jumped at me from Tinkle's hand and the room exploded with sound.

I dropped to one knee, snapped off a lightning shot at Tinkle as I saw his gun leveling at me; I pulled the trigger once more and saw him stagger, but his gun boomed again and I felt the slap of a bullet against my left hand; the impact of that heavy slug spun me halfway around, the light tumbling to the floor and going out. I went down on both knees, forcing my gun hand back toward Tinkle, twisting my body and snapping a wild shot at him, then getting the gun barrel centered on his chest and firing twice so fast the shots blurred into one sound.

He started falling as I saw Artie's hand digging under his coat, coming out with a snub-nosed revolver, but Artie never got the gun an inch away from his chest because I shot him in the head. Dimly I saw his body go limp, but like a crazy man I fired at him again, and heard the hammer fall on an empty cartridge. It was suddenly dark, but I triggered the gun still again, not even realizing the chambers were empty, not comprehending the darkness. I was like a man in a trance, sweat drenching my body and the taste of blood on my lips where I'd bitten them, the smell of cordite in my nostrils, and the drumming of blood in my brain.

I was still on my knees, body twisted, pain obvious in my left hand now, and the quiet, the stillness seemed slowly to become like a pressure against my eardrums, and the darkness, a solid black, was like a wall around me. I got

my feet under me, stood up. Cannon wouldn't have a gun;
Cannon—

My hand touched the light switch. I slid the glasses up
off my eyes, looked toward the spot where the two men
lay on the floor, flipped on the light. I was staring to my
right as brilliant light blazed in the room and looking
there was what damn near got me killed.

It was the grunt that saved me, the fact that Cannon
always grunted before he swung that roundhouse cannonball of his, and when I heard the sound close by me on
my left I didn't even stop to turn my head. I just let my
knees go slack, dropping my body and turning as I fell,
then tensed the muscles in my legs and let them start
springing me up again as an arm that looked two yards
long whistled over my skull.

And I guess Cannon must have been surprised, because
always before when he'd swung at me it had been so
simple to hit my head, and he was all splayed out in the
air with his thick belly floating where I wanted it.

I just kept on going up, my right fist already balled
and traveling in the right direction, and I let it go and
felt it smash into his belly, heard the breath spurt from his
mouth. I swung a little farther around, then pivoted, cock-
ing my left fist and launching it at him. I knew I had him.
He was bent over, gasping, the whole side of his long
bony face bare and unprotected.

My left clipped his chin, the pain almost killing me, and
he spun halfway around, dropping to one knee. He was
down, a long way less than my size now, and I took half
a step toward him, my right hand stretching for the ceiling, and when I slammed its edge down on the base
of his skull it was easy for me to kick him in the face when
he hit the floor and rolled over on his back. So I kicked
him in the face. His jaw jerked far to the side, as if his
face were made of rubber, then sagged and hung at an
angle that was not normal at all.

I just stood there and looked at them all for a long
minute. I noticed that Tinkle's oddly humped body was
sprawled over the light he'd been holding, blotting out its
beam, and I noticed that all of the men were dressed
entirely in black; but it didn't mean anything to me. I
could have noticed that they had purple horns growing
out of their heads and it wouldn't have meant anything

to me. I wasn't in very good shape at the moment. That was all right. The rest of these guys were in terrible condition.

Finally it occurred to me that there must be a phone around here somewhere. I started looking.

9.

IT WAS four o'clock in the morning before I'd passed through Homicide, Burglary, and Scientific Investigation. I was standing on the Main Street steps of City Hall, blinking as a final flash bulb went off in my face. One of the reporters—Bruce Ladd of the *Examiner*—said, "Infrared, huh? Make quite a story. That was Payne's contribution?"

"Yeah," I said wearily. "That part was the Professor's idea; Cannon was top man, the muscle; Tinkle cased the spots and unlocked and locked the doors."

"How about that Tinkle?" another asked. "He gonna croak?"

"Slugs in his chest and stomach, but they think he'll live. He might as well croak; Cannon broke that attorney's neck, but Drake hadn't kicked off when Tinkle's bullet killed him."

"The loot?"

"Got most of it. They were holding most of the rocks till they cooled, but that part got rumbled tonight along with the rest of it. You'll have to see Captain Masterson to find out what stuff his boys picked up."

There were a few more questions from the reporters. I answered them, practically swaying on my feet. It seemed that I hadn't slept for a month. But I could sleep now; Cannon had been willing to tell the whole story, but if he moved his jaw a half inch there was a chance it would fall off, so he wrote it all down. That was nice, because it gave the boys upstairs a handwritten confession—including the fact that Cannon had rounded up Tinkle and Artie last night, after he'd left Lois and before they stole my Cad, then picked up little Joe and worked him over before their "hit-and-run" finished him.

The reporters finally had all they needed. I knew most of them, nice enough guys. The other stories about me had simply been part of their jobs, just as this tonight had been part of mine. And when one of them finally said, "Anything to add, Scott?" I nodded.

"Yeah, boys. One thing. Be sure you make it clear about Joseph Raspberry." Then they took off. They knew what I meant; they'd take care of it.

My hand was bandaged, and though I damn near lost a thumb, I'd keep the thumb, the hand, and a fat scar. All I needed was three days of sleep. And I wanted everything cleared up before I hit the sack, because I was going to lock the door and jerk the phone out of the wall. So I found a phone and called Diane, to get the whole thing wrapped up and off my mind.

Her voice was sleepy. " 'Lo?"

"Diane? Shell—Scotty, to you."

"Oh, Scotty. What's the matter?"

"Nothing. You'll get your stuff back; just wanted to let you know. It all got settled tonight."

"You darling, I knew you'd get my pretties. Are you going to bring them to me?"

Her voice didn't sound sleepy any more. Funny thing, I didn't feel quite so sleepy myself. I said, "Well . . . I don't know. Cops'll have them for a while."

"You bring them to me. I want you to."

"I suppose."

"Scotty. Are you going to sneak in like they did, and put them on my dresser?"

For a moment I thought fiendishly that maybe I should do just that: clap on my glasses, click on my monstrous red flashlight and tiptoe into her bedroom crying "Where are you-ou? Diane, where are you?" eyeballing her frantically all the while. But I said, "We'll—we'll see. But the stuff will be tied up for a while."

"Well, when it gets untied, you just bring it right out here to me."

"Okay. Good night, Diane. Let Osborne know about it. He owes me some money."

"I will. 'Bye, Daddy."

I was clear back in the Cad and rolling down Sunset before I realized what she'd called me, but I kept the car under control. That made me think about Lois. I figured she'd be in bed, too, but probably I should call her. She might be worried—and anyway, I knew now she'd never conned me, had gone along with me all the way. I pulled into a gas station and gave her a ring. She answered in five seconds.

"Hi," I said. After a little chatter I gave her a fast
rundown on the night's developments, then said, "I didn't
know if you'd still be up."

"I've been awake all night. Waiting for you to call.
You said you'd see me." I started to tell her that I was
falling asleep in the booth, but she said, "You promised,
you know. Can't you come up for one little drink?"

"I'm pretty beat—"

"I thought you'd want to come up for a nightcap, at
least, so I bought us something lovely. Can't you come
up for just one little drink?"

"You and your drinks," I said. "What color is it this
time?"

She didn't answer.

I could feel my jaw slowly sagging as a pleasantly staggering thought struck me. I said, "Honey, Lois, uh,
sweetie . . . uh, sweetie . . . uh . . ."

She said softly, "I went to so much trouble, bought us
something and put it in the refrigerator—"

"In the refrigerator?"

"—and I've been sitting here so long in this chilly old
room—"

"Chilly?"

"—and I'm so lonesome—and cold—and—"

I said, "Baby, loosen up. What the hell have you got in
that refrigerator?"

"Champagne. A whole magnum of champagne."

Man, let me tell you. I was *wide* awake. "Baby," I said,
"unlock the door and stand aside," and then I hung up
and trotted for the Cad. What the hell, I was thinking.
One little drink never hurt anybody. Anyway not too
much.

❖❖❖❖❖❖❖❖❖❖❖❖❖❖❖❖

*A powerful and moving story of six young soldiers,
scared, brave, bone-weary . . . and utterly real
by a man who was there*

STEVEN N. SPETZ
RAT PACK SIX

FTA—three little letters expressing GI despair and disillu-
sion, scratched and chalked everywhere you look in war-torn
Vietnam.

FTA—how does it feel to have your whole life boiled down
into one latrine-wall motto?

Ask the Rat Pack—The Rat, Ski, Chigro, Pancho, the Owl
and Steve. See life as they see it—close up in the cruddy,
bloody, jungle war that seems to have no meaning, no cause,
no end in sight. The Rat Pack and their little friend, Le
Quang, will bring the Vietnam war home to you as nothing
ever has.

R2182   *A Fawcett* Gold Medal Book   60¢

Wherever Paperbacks Are Sold

Joe Gall Masquerades As A Soul
Brother In A Secret Army Of Assassins

THE TREMBLING EARTH CONTRACT

Philip Atlee

Joe Gall—Color him black for contract #10

Even a steel-nerved expert in sudden death like Joe Gall could hardly be expected to take on a whole army. But that's exactly what this contract demanded.

A secret organization of black militants had molded itself into a ruthless, highly trained guerrilla army. Inflamed by centuries of white injustice, they had already begun to terrorize the South. Their ultimate objective was a complete take-over. They had to be stopped. Quickly. And silently.

All Joe Gall needed was a few injections, an Afro wig, phony identification, a prison record—and presto!—Joe Gall, white secret agent, became John Earle, black secret soldier.

2181   *A Fawcett Gold Medal Book*   60¢

Wherever Paperbacks Are Sold

If your dealer is sold out, send cover price plus 10¢ each for postage and handling to Gold Medal Books, Fawcett Publications, Inc., Greenwich, Conn. 06830. If order is for five or more books, there is no postage or handling charge. Order by number and title. No Canadian orders.

GREAT BESTSELLERS
FROM THE PUBLISHER OF
MANDINGO

THE BLACK SUN (*with Kyle Onstott*)
M1724   95

THE MAHOUND   M2179   95

ROGUE ROMAN   T1978   75

THE STREET OF THE SUN   M2048   95

THE TATTOOED ROOD (*with Kyle Onstott*)
M1053   95

. . . five bestsellers by LANCE HORNER in the tremendous storytelling tradition that has blistered the American literary scene for the last decade.

FAWCETT WORLD LIBRARY
Wherever Paperbacks Are Sold